FANDOM TO FANTASY
VOLUME 1

FANDOM TO FANTASY
VOLUME 1

EDITED BY
ISABELLA
&
SALLYANNE MONTI

SAPPHIRE BOOKS

SALINAS, CALIFORNIA

Fandom to Fantasy - Volume 1
Copyright © 2018 by Sapphire Authors. All rights reserved.

ISBN - 978-1-948232-18-0

This is a work of fiction - names, characters, places, and incidents are the product of the author's imagination or are used fictitiously. Any resemblance to actual persons living or dead, business, events or locales is entirely coincidental.

Editors - Isabella & Sallyanne Monti
Cover design - Fantasy Book Designs
Book design - LJ Reynolds

Sapphire Books Publishing, LLC
P.O. Box 8142
Salinas, CA 93912
www.sapphirebooks.com

Printed in the United States of America
First Edition – April 2018

This and other Sapphire Books titles can be found at
www.sapphirebooks.com

Dedication

This book is dedicated to the visionaries who create a rich tapestry of stories that reflect a world as it could be, not as it is.

Long live the dreamers!

Isabella

Isabella's Acknowledgments

Thank you to Ljilja for taking a few images and creating a masterpiece. I always see the vision, but you bring the covers to life.

To Sallyanne, LJ Ryenolds, Peggy Adams and all the other who make this work possible. This couldn't happen without you.

Isabella

Acknowledgments

This anthology series is a compilation of creative contributions from a innovate group of writers who bring their imagination, and unique storytelling to life, in the pages of this book.

Thank you, to our partner ClexaCon, who joined forces with Sapphire Books to promote the call for submissions, and for hosting the book release party at ClexaCon2018, in Las Vegas, NV, April 2018.

Thank you, to the authors who entrusted us with their original bodies of work.

Thank you, Fantasy Book Designs for bringing the cover art to life, and LJ Reynolds for leading the details with superior book design and layout.

Thank you, Sapphire Books and Publisher Christine Svendsen, for creating a welcoming space for literary artists to construct exceptional projects.

It's a privilege to collaborate with all the talented professionals who brought this project to life, and an honor to represent the exceptional bodies of work. Anthologies are a dream come true for this short story fanatic.

Dare to Dream!
Sallyanne Monti, Editor

Table of Contents

The Apology

By Anna Gram

To say Melanie was pissed off was an understatement. The humiliation she endured on set was enough to drive her to drink the beer waiting for her in the fridge at home. Melanie thought long and hard. She could say it was the heat. Whoever thought it was smart to shoot a film in the middle of summer didn't read weather reports, even if they were in Maine. But she couldn't blame the weather any more than she could blame herself. What happened today was based solely on status, the hierarchy that exists during film production, and the realization that no matter how close you are to someone that status will never change.

Melanie, or Mel to her friends, was excited when she first heard they were producing a film in her home state. She was looking forward to being in her old stomping grounds and seeing all that changed. She lucked out landing this gig, not only for the location but also because of who was starring in this little Indy production.

Sarah Williams. The greatest actress Mel had ever seen. The only actress Mel found attractive. She was working with her for three months, and she was in charge of Sarah's microphone. She had been an admirer of Sarah's work for a long time, and an admirer of a few other attributes of hers that had nothing to do with her talent. Mel was excited, and she told a few of her friends, some of whom had worked with Sarah in the past. They weren't very kind when talking about Sarah.

"She's more than a diva," they warned. "She's the fucking evil queen incarnate." Usually, Mel heeded her friends' warnings when it came to difficult actors, but she had stars in her eyes when she looked at Sarah. Mel didn't put too much stock in their cautionary tales.

After the first day, Mel thought maybe she should've listened to their advice. It wasn't the introduction she was hoping for, but all things considered, Mel knew it could've been worse. She went around distributing the microphones to the actors, intentionally saving Sarah's mic for last because Mel knew she could linger and in the hopes, Sarah would talk to her. That was Mel's first mistake. As soon as she knocked on Sarah's trailer door and announced who she was, Sarah yanked the door open, yelling. "Where the hell have you been?" Along with a string of profanities, Sarah quickly snatched the microphone out of Mel's hand.

Mel dropped her stargazing demeanor, and immediately went into professional mode. It was something she didn't often do unless she was dealing with a demanding actor. Mel liked things to be laidback, She stepped up on the trailer step, grabbed Sarah's wrist firmly, and stopped within an inch from her face.

"Look. I know you're the star of this film. And you like to have things done a certain way. If you tell me what they are, I will do my best to accommodate those needs. But if you ever snatch a microphone out of my hand like that again, I will make sure you have to redo every line you utter on this project. Are we clear?"

Mel saw a flash of something primal in Sarah's eyes before she slowly nodded her acceptance. She let go of her hand, walked back down the steps, and left Sarah standing there staring after her. They didn't speak for a few days. It was a little too icy for Mel's liking. They didn't have any other issues. Well, they didn't have many. They still butted heads over a few things about settings and placement, which was common when working with a new person and learning the other person's preferences and quirks. But since their initial meeting, Sarah was respectful and not the hot mess that Mel observed on that first day. It was as if Mel's retort had endeared her to Sarah, earning Sarah's respect in a way. It also made Mel think that maybe this evil queen personae that Sarah was so well known for was just a façade that she felt she had to put on for the world to see. Or Sarah just liked the idea of someone standing up to her. Whatever the reason, it caused a shift in their relationship.

One night, three weeks into the shoot, Mel and Sarah were sitting outside enjoying the balmy night air after they had wrapped for the day. They hadn't socialized much until then, so Mel was happy to have the opportunity to learn about Sarah and vice versa. Mel learned Sarah's mother had pushed her into acting. Her father left when she was a child but was always there for her accomplishments. Mel told her about growing up in foster care and suggested Sarah might be thankful to have a family that cares about her, even if it wasn't in the traditional sense.

When they finally called it a night, Sarah said, "Thank you for sharing yourself with me."

And when Mel turned to respond, she saw that same primal look in Sarah's eyes that she'd seen on that first day. Sarah kissed her. What followed was a night of passion. Their mouths discovered sensitive spots behind their knees and inside of wrists. Soft fingertips explored the sensuality inside, bringing each other to the edge over and over again before falling into the abyss of desire. It was a night full of carnal discovery. Mel couldn't look at Sarah the next day without blushing.

Unfortunately, as the heat in their relationship started to rise, so did the heat of the Maine summer.

In hindsight, Mel should've seen it coming. Three days after she and Sarah began their off-set activities, the schedule called for a series of outdoor shots. It was one of the hottest days of the year when they started the filming sequence. After the first day, everyone felt tired, sweaty, dirty, and snippy. Transporters couldn't deliver the climate-controlled trailers to the set for cast and crew. The unpaved roads were too risky for the expensive equipment. Instead, the producer brought in tents for shade, which made the whole day unbearable.

By the second day, the heat started wreaking havoc on Mel's sound equipment. While she wrapped the mic packs beforehand to keep them dry, the actors excessive sweating broke through the waterproof barriers time and again. Mel was constantly on the move to replace the packs before the moisture reached the interiors. She finally decided to keep the packs with her until the last possible second to make sure they stayed dry and to get the maximum performance out of them. Sarah was sweating more profusely than everyone else, and ten minutes after securing her microphone, Mel heard signs of damage over her headphones. She immediately ran and grabbed Sarah's pack, pulling out the drenched microphone.

By this point, the heat was making everyone short-tempered. Sarah's evil queen personae erupted with a vengeance. No one was safe from her wrath, not even Mel.

Mel grabbed the replacement pack out of her utility belt, but the connection to the mic was temperamental, so it took a little extra finessing. When she finally freed the mic, Mel immediately plugged it into the new pack and positioned it back on Sarah's costume. While the director and the rest of the crew were frustrated standing in the middle of the scorching sun waiting, they understood these things happen.

Sarah didn't deal with the delay as calmly. Mel didn't reprimand Sarah when she ripped the microphone out of her hand. Nor did she utter a word when Sarah yelled at her.

"Why can't you do your fucking job?" with the entire cast and crew nearby. What happened next, made Mel fume.

After getting the equipment positioned on Sarah, she walked back to her station and put on her headphones to sound check Sarah's mic. Mel was stunned at what she was hearing. Sarah, the famous Hollywood actress, was berating the work of Mel, the lowly sound tech to another actor. It wasn't until Sarah finished her tirade that she looked up and saw Mel with the headphones on. She knew Mel had heard every word. Mel thought she saw a flash of fear cross Sarah's face, but it was soon masked by Sarah's film persona, as the director said "places everyone" and "action."

When they finally wrapped for the day, Mel packed up her gear as quickly as possible. With hotter temperatures predicted, the director and the producer decided to give everyone the next two days off. Mel got her orders and left, hoping her bruised ego and angry mood would cool off in the two days away from Sarah.

Mel arrived home and quickly showered the dirt and grime away. Unfortunately, she had left the air conditioning off all day, and it was hot inside. She sat on the outdoor deck waiting for the house to cool down, drinking beer and accumulating an impressive collection of empty bottles. Mel knew she could've gone down to the Holiday Inn to hang with the crew and enjoy the free air conditioning. But she thought the risk of running into Sarah was too high, and she just couldn't handle that…not with her blood still boiling.

Her phone chirped at her for about an hour with text messages and voicemails before going silent. She knew it wasn't any of the crew. They only communicated by email. Mel knew who it was, and she knew why she was calling. Mel didn't expect to hear from her until the next day. She was mildly impressed. Regardless, she wasn't ready to listen to what Sarah had to say.

That's how Melanie found herself sitting in the mesh fabric lawn chair on a broken-down patio, with her head tilted back, her eyes closed, her long blond hair falling over the back of the chair while listening to the crickets and cicadas in the yard. The heat hadn't dissipated much since the sun went down, and she could already feel a light sheen of sweat forming on her clean skin, making her feel hot and sticky all over again.

Mel adjusted her position in the chair trying to get more comfortable. She uncrossed her legs to let them dangle off the edge, causing a rustle in the chair's fabric. It sounded oddly loud over the insect activity in the yard, but not louder than the sound of the creaking door hinge as the latch on the backyard gate was lifted. She listened as the dry grass shuffled out of the way of the gate's path. Soft footsteps walked through the foliage, and the stress of the boards creaked as someone stepped onto the deck.

Mel didn't open her eyes. She didn't have to.

"I've been calling you." Sarah's tone held no guilt or remorse. It just sounded authoritative.

"I'm not ready to talk to you," Mel said.

Sarah sighed heavily. "Mel…"

She held up a finger and stopped whatever Sarah planned to say. It was a firm gesture and left no room for argument. The boards creaked again under the weight of Sarah's footsteps as she moved further onto the deck. Finally succumbing to curiosity, Mel opened her eyes and looked at her.

She couldn't talk, even if she wanted to. Overcome by the sexy vision before her. Sarah was wearing a tight-fitting, short-sleeved, button-down plaid shirt that strained against her breasts. She paired it with the tiniest cut-off shorts Mel had ever seen, accenting her favorite feature, Sarah's legs. She finished off the ensemble with a simple pair of flip-flops. Her dark, luscious hair, usually flowing freely over Sarah's shoulders, was pulled back into a tight ponytail sitting on top of her head, highlighting her long, gorgeous neck.

The other night, they revealed some of their fantasies to each other, picking and choosing the ones they would like to explore. Sarah took a particular interest in a specific one. Mel had told her about the fantasy she had of a woman dressed in a tight flannel shirt and short shorts, straddling Mel's lap and having her way with Mel in a hayloft. Sarah seemed intrigued by it. And judging by the outfit she had chosen to wear for her visit, she remembered every detail Mel told her.

If she came to apologize, she's on the right track

for me to accept it, Mel thought.

"Why didn't you answer my calls?" Sarah asked.

Mel blinked a couple of times, shaking away the fantasy caused by the eye candy standing before her. *I am angry with her,* Mel thought, *and I have to remember that.*

"I'm sorry," Mel replied, her voice dripping with sarcasm. "I'm just an incompetent sound tech who doesn't know how to work an on/off switch. So how can I possibly be expected to know how to work a simple thing like a phone?"

Sarah looked down at her shoes, shame clouding her expression. "I deserve that," she murmured.

"Damn right you do!" Mel's anger seeped back in, and her voice began to rise. The humiliation and embarrassment she endured earlier returned full force. Sexy outfit damned, she needed to say this.

"You not only humiliated me in front of everyone within the broadcast radius of that frequency but the actor you criticized me to, is going to make my job ten times more difficult because he thinks it's all true! And what pisses me off is, it's all bullshit! You know what I do is a lot of hard work! An entire evening of talking and sharing, and today it's like it was nothing to you! So, excuse me if I don't feel like accepting your apology right now." Mel's words echoed off the deck and disappeared into the darkness. In the distance, a dog barked in response, reflecting just how far Mel's anger reached.

She slumped back down into the chair, let out a frustrated sigh and closed her eyes again. She was physically and emotionally exhausted and just wanted Sarah to say what she came to say and leave. She liked Sarah, a lot, but at this point, Mel just wanted to be left alone.

It was quiet for so long, Mel thought Sarah had left until she felt the slightest brush against her right leg. It was fleeting at first, but then it returned, with more pressure. She suddenly felt the same sensation on her left leg, soft yet firm. Mel didn't have to see her to know what was going on and what Sarah was doing. The heat and the beers, heightened by the anger coursing through her veins caused Mel's body to betray her. She opened her eyes and saw Sarah standing above her, straddling her legs. Sarah stared at her, not saying a word, and Mel could read her expression and the fire that had become so recognizable, in Sarah's eyes. Mel knew she wouldn't be able to hold out for long. She was happy Sarah wanted to apologize, but Mel wasn't sure about the tactics she was using.

Sarah lowered herself, settling gently on Mel's lap. It took all of Mel's energy to stifle the moan that wanted to escape. Sarah saw the strain on Mel's face and smiled. She wasn't playing fair, and she knew it, but Sarah also knew she was far from a victory.

"I am deeply sorry for my comments today, Mel," she whispered. "I could say it was the heat or the long day, but I don't want to give you flimsy excuses that I know you won't, and shouldn't, believe. What I said was wrong, no matter what the conditions were. I shouldn't have directed it at someone I've come to care about, deeply. That hurts even more." She paused to gauge Mel's reaction. She was reluctant to give too much away, so Mel stayed neutral until Sarah finished her statement.

"As for any problems from the cast or crew doubting your abilities," she continued, "You don't have to worry about that. I made sure that all of the parties involved know that you are a skilled professional who takes her job and position seriously and knows exactly what she is doing."

The air was thick with humidity and desire, and it was making it hard to breathe. Mel cleared her throat.

"Thank you. I appreciate you doing that."

Mel's voice was husky. Sarah must have heard it too because she began to execute a light touch of fingertips, stroking Mel's forearms. She was trying to coax Mel into forgiving her, and Mel's willpower was waning, even more so when Sarah upped the ante and started to press feather-light kisses against her neck.

"Do you forgive me?" she asked in between kisses.

Mel huffed out a frustrated laugh in response.

"What am I supposed to do? Accept your apology and let you have your way with me?"

Sarah stopped her kisses, cupped Mel's face and turned her head to meet Sarah's gaze. "No," she said matter-of-factly. "So you can have your way with me."

Suddenly it dawned on Mel the entire point of this visit. The skimpy outfit that was right out of her fantasy, the hairstyle she knew was Mel's favorite, and the way Sarah had positioned them in the chair. It was all planned, calculated down to the last physical detail. Sarah wasn't there to speak an apology. She was the apology.

Sarah leaned in for a kiss, but Mel turned her head and dodged the effort. Sarah tried again, but Mel turned the opposite way. When Sarah made a third attempt, Mel grabbed her by the wrists, yanked her hands away and held them between their bodies, close to her chest. Sarah gasped at the forceful action, a tinge of surprise and fear passing over her eyes, hinting at her desire.

"Don't touch me," Mel commanded, and she tightened her grip for emphasis. Sarah looked disappointed and confused, afraid Mel was going to send her away. Mel resolved these feelings by loosening her grip just a bit and not letting go. She gently pulled Sarah's hands apart and maneuvered them until they were behind Mel's head. She slid her hands to meet Sarah's hands and unclenched her fists, encouraging Sarah to grab the mesh of the chair. Once she secured Sarah's hands to the fabric, Mel squeezed them lightly, leaned forward and placed her lips next to Sarah's ear.

"No matter what happens," she whispered seductively, "don't let go, and don't you dare move from this position."

When she saw the slight nod of understanding from Sarah, she let go, and her hands began to travel up Sarah's forearms—slowly, methodically. Mel felt a light shiver course through Sarah's body, as the goosebumps formed under her touch, despite the sweltering heat. As her hands continued up towards Sarah's collarbone, her gaze followed the same path. She couldn't resist touching the exposed flesh that Sarah's shirt revealed at her neckline. She focused on a small bead of sweat, trickling down Sarah's neck, its destination ultimately the valley between her breasts. Mel raised a finger and followed the path like an explorer. She loved the sharp intake of breath she heard come from Sarah as a result of her actions. It was enough to bring a coy smile to her lips as her finger suddenly stopped between Sarah's breasts with the lightest of touches.

If this were any other night, any other scenario, Mel would've given in to desire and put both of them out of their misery, but she wanted to take her time. She wanted Sarah to understand what it meant to give an apology.

Every ounce of negative emotion was replaced by pure lust, as Mel locked her gaze with Sarah's. Sarah's body started to hum with anticipation. Mel slowly worked her way down over the barrier of clothes to the exposed skin of Sarah's thighs, which had surprisingly increased as her shorts rose up. She didn't stop there, though. She lightly grazed her fingernails over Sarah's legs and under the hem of her shorts. It was a highly sensitive area Mel had discovered recently. She could feel Sarah's muscles contract under her fingertips, and her whimpered response was exactly what Mel was hoping.

With her hands busy, Mel started taking advantage of Sarah's exposed neck. The sheen of sweat glistening there, along with the scent of Sarah's fruity bath wash was enough to make Mel lean forward and place deep, open-mouth kisses along her collarbone, tasting whatever that unique blend was on her body. She could tell by the soft moans, Sarah was enjoying this torture.

Still, she didn't move.

The kissing was enough of a distraction that Sarah couldn't keep track of Mel's hands. They had changed course and moved further down to the bottom hem of Sarah's shirt. Once they reached their destination, Mel pulled back from Sarah's neck. Sarah moaned in protest at the loss of contact.

"Is this shirt new?"

Sarah nodded.

Mel smiled wickedly. "Not anymore," she said just before she yanked the lapels apart, ripping the fabric, and sending buttons clattering across the deck and echoing into the night. It was a sound Mel would never forget. Sarah looked into Mel's eyes. Her breath was shallow, almost to the point of panting. Mel knew what she wanted, but this was Sarah's apology to her, so Mel was taking her time to do as she pleased. *When I have to apologize to her, Sarah can do whatever she wants at whatever pace she wants. Tonight, she is mine.*

Mel raised her finger to Sarah's throat and repeated the path she started earlier taking full advantage of the exposed skin. Gliding slowly, Mel passed the collarbone, down between Sarah's breasts and continued further until she reached the top of Sarah's shorts. She grazed the back of her hand lightly across Sarah's abdomen, feeling her muscles contract and shiver at her touch. She could hear Sarah's soft moans. It was a telltale sign that Sarah was close. Mel had never known anyone to come from being caressed, but she was willing to put this theory to test, just not tonight.

Somewhere during Mel's journey, Sarah had closed her eyes tightly. A slight rhythm started in the movement of Sarah's hips as she concentrated on the sensations Mel was causing. Mel wanted Sarah to see what she was about to do to her, so she stopped.

"Open your eyes," Mel whispered. Sarah reluctantly complied. Mel wrapped her arms around her, pulling Sarah more securely onto her lap, Sarah's breathing still ragged. She wanted Sarah hard and tight against her, while Mel continued to caress her.

Sarah felt the reaction this seduction was having on Mel. While she appeared calm and in control on the outside, inside Mel's heart was racing and threatening to beat out of her chest.

Mel leaned into her as if she was about to kiss her. Sarah leaned into her as well, expecting their lips to meet finally. Mel moved her head to the side at the last moment and planted her mouth on Sarah's neck, the spot just below her ear that drove her crazy. Sarah buried her face into Mel's neck muffling the moan that threatened to escape. She let out a sharp breath against Mel's shoulder. Mel couldn't tell if it was out of arousal or frustration. She heard Sarah whisper.

"You're driving me crazy wanting to kiss you." Mel smiled, realizing she had her answer. Sarah was aroused.

Mel stopped long enough to say, "This is for me. I'll do what I like when I like."

Sarah's eyes went black with desire at her tone. She began to whimper and moved her hips again, trying to get Mel to come closer.

Mel returned her mouth to Sarah's neck, sucking hard, branding Sarah as her own. She could tell it was becoming unbearable for Sarah, judging by the sound of the twisting fabric behind her head. Mel trailed light kisses across Sarah's collarbone and down to her breasts. When she pushed the bra cup aside and took one beautifully aroused nipple into her mouth, Mel heard the fabric almost tear in two from Sarah's twisted grip. Sarah was itching to touch Mel, to push her head down to her breast and guide Mel to where she needed her touch.

As her mouth lavished attention on first one breast then the other, Mel's hands expertly unbuttoned Sarah's shorts. The sound of the opening zipper was audibly loud as it broke through their lustful haze. Mel rested her hands on Sarah's waist, leaving the shorts open. She gasped as she looked down and noticed Sarah wasn't wearing any underwear. It was almost enough to send Mel into a frenzy. She was ready to accept this apology, but not quite yet.

Mel pulled away and looked up to find Sarah's

face contorted and her eyes closed. With her left hand, Mel cupped Sarah's face and silently urged her to open her eyes and look at her. When she finally did, Mel saw passion and love. She took a minute to admire it. She stroked her thumb across Sarah's bottom lip, caressing the plump flesh. Sarah's right hand moved behind Mel's head along the back of the chair, her hands straining against the fabric. With a gentle caress on Sarah's forearms, Mel coaxed her to let go and wrap her hands around Mel's neck. It wouldn't take long to send Sarah over the edge, and she wanted her anchored to her when it happened.

Without so much as a preamble or warning, Mel pushed her right hand into Sarah's shorts, finding no resistance and a lot of wetness. She stroked Sarah's outer lips and circled her clit lightly. It wasn't enough to send her flying, but it was enough to get her attention. Sarah looked into Mel's eyes, gasping for air, never wavering her gaze.

"You are so wet," Mel gasped. "Is that because of me?"

Mel changed her pattern, pushing one finger in just a little bit, causing a gasp to escape out into the night.

"It's...you," Sarah stuttered, digging her nails into Mel's scalp. "It's always because of you."

This was the exact response Mel wanted. She didn't want to prolong this anymore. She needed to make Sarah come, make her come hard, and then start all over again in the comfort of her bedroom. As quickly as she could, she added a second finger and plunged them deep inside. The response was instantaneous, and Sarah came hard and fast, the effects seeping all over Mel's hand. Before Sarah could make a sound,

Mel covered Sarah's mouth with her own and initiated the most passionate kiss she could as she swallowed Sarah's scream of ecstasy.

She didn't remove her hand from Sarah's shorts, or her mouth from hers until she came back down. Mel could tell right away when that moment happened because Sarah started kissing her in the most tender and loving way. After what felt like hours, their lips parted for air. Sarah pressed her forehead against Mel's as she pulled her hand out of Sarah's shorts and wrapped her arms firmly around her waist. They sat there in silence, surrounded by nothing but the sound of crickets and cicadas, and the humid summer night as they waited for their breathing to return to normal.

When their breathing was even, Sarah pulled back enough to look into Mel's eyes. There was such tenderness there, and the hunger Mel loved to see, directed towards her.

"Does this mean you forgive me?" Sarah asked.

Mel didn't say anything. She tightened her hold on Sarah and quickly stood up. Sarah tightened her grip on Mel's neck and wrapped her legs around her waist. As Mel walked towards the door leading to the interior of the house, she kissed Sarah passionately once again and said, "I accept your apology. But can I forgive you in the morning?"

Anna Gram works as a sound editor and music editor at Sony Picture Entertainment in Los Angeles, CA. She also writes book reviews for The Lesbian Review website. When she's not working, she's reading, writing, playing softball, or trying to find ways to make the world better.

The Promise

By Kim Pritekel

Rya Leonard wiped her hands on her apron after she moved all the sugar, salt, and pepper shakers off the breakfast counter.

"Why would I want to do that?" she asked, eying her friend, Shelby, who was wiping down tables on the other side of the small diner. Business came to a crawl after a robust lunch rush.

"Maybe because you were obsessed with the show back in the day?" Shelby said, standing erect as she rose from bending over a four-top. She grimaced as she leaned slightly backward to stretch her back. "Damn, hurting today."

"Sorry, Shel," Rya said, dunking her rag in Lysol water before she began wiping the counter. "I *was* obsessed, not *am* obsessed, don't you think?"

Rya rolled her hazel eyes when she saw Shelby walking over to her, her dark blonde eyebrow arched. Shelby reached over the counter pulling the sleeve of Rya's uniform, exposing her right shoulder.

"And, for the woman who has already planned her funeral, I guess getting the 'Bailer B' tattooed on your skin was a spontaneous decision?"

Rya batted Shelby's hand away as she returned to her work, saying nothing.

"I was there, remember?" Shelby reminded, also

returning to her work. "It meant a lot to you when we were twenty-four, and I know it means a lot to you now. Besides," she added, hand on her rounded hip, "When do we do anything fun?"

Rya was quiet for a moment as she tossed the idea around in her head along with the pros and cons.

"Who all is going to be there?" she asked finally.

"Well, Jason Portney, of course. I mean, you can't exactly have a reunion Con of *The Bailers* without Conrad Bailer himself. Uh, the guy who played the dad, oh, what was his name?"

"Winston Eddy," Rya murmured, beginning to wipe down the sugar shakers.

"The mom and older sister..." Shelby said.

"Anita Faulkner and Tina Yammer..."

Shelby met Rya's quick gaze for a moment, the Hispanic woman looking to be deep in thought before her dark, exotic eyes flashed to Rya again.

"And, I think the younger sister, too."

Rya let out a heavy sigh, reaching over to grab the salt and pepper shakers for their wipe down as she said, "Jenny Jacobs." She glanced up when she saw that Shelby had walked over to the breakfast counter again. "What?"

"Come on, Rya," the restaurant manager's oldest friend said, pleading in her voice. "You can still remember their real names. Let's go and have some fun."

She gave Rya her famous devilish Shelby Hernandez smile.

"Don't forget your promise."

Rya gave her a sheepish grin.

"Yeah, the promise of a twenty-one-year-old kid who said meeting the Bailers was on her bucket list."

"Exactly. Well, here's your chance."

⚝⚝⚝⚝

Taking several deep breaths, Rya stood in the women's restroom, hands resting on the edge of one of the sinks as she looked at her reflection in the mirror. She wore her dark brown hair in a short, sporty cut, as it was too wavy to manage long. Expressive hazel eyes looked back at her, noting feminine features and slightly arched eyebrows.

Letting out a heavy sigh, she pushed away and garnered the courage to head back to the convention. Shelby was waiting for her outside the restroom, as her son called just as they were about to enter the bathroom.

"Everything okay?" Shelby asked, leaning a shoulder against the wall of the hotel's hallway, the large room where the convention was being held a few doors down.

"I was going to ask the same of you," Rya said, wiping her sweating palms on her jeans as they made their way to the festivities.

"Yup. Kyle checked in on your kittens twice and, everything is good."

"Okay, good," Rya said.

She felt as if she was about to vomit. Even though she managed a popular downtown diner, she wasn't the social type. With so many people around, she felt overwhelmed. Rya had to admit. It was also the thought of seeing her in person.

The convention was in full swing once she and Shelby arrived. Rya wasn't surprised to see a bunch of men and women her age wandering around, considering the show had run from 1995 to 2001, beginning just after Rya had graduated high school. She was pleased to see younger generations in attendance.

The series featured a young scientist, Conrad Bailer, who created a time machine and inadvertently sent his entire family scattered through time. The plot continued as he picked up the pieces and family members, over the run of the show. It wasn't surprising to see people walking around dressed in the various costumes from the places and times where episodes and adventures had taken place.

Shelby tried to get her to dress up, but Rya shyly opted to dress in well-fitted jeans and a casual, women's cut button-down shirt. She felt relatively confident as she and Shelby made their way through the crowds of talking, laughing and excited convention goers. There were various booths set up with vendors selling DVD sets, props from the show, signed and unsigned photographs, and additional booths where fans can meet the actors.

"Damn, that line is crazy long at the table with all the actors," Shelby pointed out. "Why don't we wander around and look at stuff? Maybe buy a poster or something."

Rya nodded her agreement, the forest of people too thick to get a good look at any of the actors.

"Hey, look!"

Rya was jostled out of her observations by an aggressive smack to her arm from Shelby. "Was that necessary?"

"Sorry. But, look!" Shelby exclaimed, smacking Rya again. "You can sign up to have lunch with your favorite star from the show, or even all of them!"

"Nah, that's okay. I don't—Shelby!" She lost

track of her heavyset friend as she disappeared into the crowd. "Shit." Looking around nervously, Rya decided to give chase and try to catch up with Shelby.

"Excuse me," she said as she bumped this person and that.

"Oh, I'm sorry, are you okay?" The woman who nearly knocked her down asked.

"Yeah, I'm fine."

She froze, looking into the turquoise eyes that had chased her right out of the closet. Before she could say another word, the woman gave her a quick smile and then disappeared into the crowd, nothing more than a vision of flowing auburn hair, a great ass encased in tight jeans and her perfume, a scent Rya would remember forever.

"Hey." Shelby had returned.

Rya continued to stare into the crowd, Shelby's greeting disregarded.

"Hello? Earth to Rya."

Rya glanced at her friend, who was on her tippy toes, apparently trying to see what had captured Rya's attention so thoroughly.

"Hi."

Shelby met her gaze, a bemused smirk on her painted lips.

"What the hell? You look like you just saw a ghost."

Rya shook herself out of her shock. "Where did you go? I told you I'd only come if you didn't leave like you usually do." Rya was angry, and she wanted Shelby to know it.

"Yeah, yeah," her friend said, sliding an arm around Rya's shoulders. "Come on, let's go get some pictures and shit for the actors to sign."

"Wait, Shelby…"

Shelby stopped and turned to her friend, grabbing both of Rya's biceps.

"Rya," she said softly, "You've got to come out of your shell. Being so afraid of the damn world isn't you." She gave her a loving smile. After thirty years of friendship, she knew her well. "You're better than that. Let yourself enjoy life for a change."

An hour later, Rya stood behind Shelby in the long line to meet the actors of the TV series and get their signature on the photographs purchased at the convention, apparently the only thing they would be signing. Rya purchased one of the entire cast for each to sign, and then, she couldn't help it and bought one of Jenny Jacobs.

"You excited?" Shelby asked, a full cast photo in her hands.

"Nervous," Rya blew out. Though she knew her friend had never been into the show like she was, she knew that anything TV or film excited and intrigued Shelby.

"Yes, I'm excited, I suppose."

Finally, they reached the table where the cast sat in a row, some standing to shake hands and briefly speak to folks, others retaining their seats the entire time, barely acknowledging the fans as they quickly scribbled a signature with Sharpies.

Rya glanced down the row to see Jenny Jacobs. Sure enough, that's who had run into her when she'd been hurrying after Shelby. Though the series had ended when Jenny Jacobs was barely twenty-three, now, as a woman nearing forty, Rya was taken aback by the stunning beauty that was the actress and youngest of the cast. Her long, auburn hair looked soft to the touch and shiny underneath all the overhead lights. She wore fitted jeans that hugged womanly hips and a cute women's flannel shirt, sleeves rolled up and the front unbuttoned just low enough to show the slightest hint of cleavage. She seemed to be kind and talkative to the fans, chatting and posing for selfies before quickly signing pictures.

"Hi!"

It took Rya a moment to realize that Jenny Jacobs was talking to her, looking at her, acknowledging her. She swallowed and brought a hand up to run through her hair as she looked into those searing turquoise eyes.

"Hi," she managed weakly.

"I'm Jenny. What's your name?"

As Jenny extended her hand towards her, Rya glanced down stupidly. She felt a bump on her shoulder and realized it was Shelby trying to get her to wake up. Clearing her throat, she took the warm, soft hand in hers.

"Rya. I'm Rya."

Jenny gave her a blinding smile. "That's an unusual and beautiful name."

"Oh." Rya gave her a shy grin. "Thanks."

"This woman was seriously obsessed with you," Shelby said while pointing to Rya and putting her arm around Rya's shoulders. "I mean, if it wasn't an episode with Esther in it, it wasn't worth watching or talking about!"

"Shelby!" Rya hissed, far too embarrassed to look at Jenny. "I'm sorry," she whispered, bringing up the hand that wasn't holding the picture, to cover her face. Rya felt mortified when she saw Jenny stand up, leave the booth, and hurry around to her, giving Rya a quick but tight hug.

"You're adorable," she murmured into her ear, then hurried back to her place, leaving a stunned Rya where she stood.

"Come on, Romeo," Shelby muttered, shoving Rya along.

"If I could have your attention, ladies, and gentleman!" a voice boomed through the speakers littering the room. "We'll be drawing for the lucky folks who get to meet with our stars!"

Rya snorted. "Yeah, like anyone wins this stuff."

❧❧❧❧

Rya sat nervously at Mario's, a casual Italian place with decent food and a chatter-friendly environment. When they called Rya's name, indicating she'd won lunch with one of the cast members, she'd nearly peed herself. Though no clue which actor would be meeting her, it should still be an interesting experience.

There she sat, tucked into a table near the window so she could see if she was being stood up or not. When the people from the convention had contacted her with details for today's lunch, she'd been glad the restaurant chosen wasn't too far from her house.

Finally, and right on time, Rya saw a face she recognized. Though she couldn't remember the name of the actress, she identified her as the woman who had played the grandmother in a handful of episodes. She wasn't sure what to talk to this woman about, but it would still be fun, she hoped. She felt her heart thumping in her chest when she saw the second cast member appear behind grandma.

Rya stood and raised a hand in greeting while getting their attention.

"Hello."

"Hi!" Jenny Jacobs exclaimed, hurrying to Rya's side of the table to give her a heartfelt hug. "It's nice to see you again, Rya. Angie," she said, turning to the older woman. "This is Rya, Rya, Angie Reynolds, a.k.a., Grandma Rose."

Rya accepted a hug from the older actress. She was distracted by the scent of Jenny's perfume and her energy. The two actresses sat across from her and, as Rya enjoyed the conversation, they spoke mostly about the show and little background stories that no other fans knew. Rya focused her attention on Jenny. She wore jeans and a lightweight emerald green sweater, bringing out more of the green in her eyes, and showing off perfect breasts and a slender torso. Rya could hardly breathe, let alone think.

The hour lunch passed quickly. Jenny paid the bill, against Rya's protests, and then the three walked out to the parking lot. Jenny parked her rental car on the opposite side of the parking lot from where Rya had parked her two-year-old black VW Bug.

"It was wonderful to meet you," the aging actress said, leaving a lipstick mark on Rya's cheek with the grandmotherly hug and kiss she gave her. "Now, it's time for my afternoon nap."

Rya smiled as she helped the older woman into the front seat. Passenger door closed, she walked around to where Jenny Jacobs stood at the driver's side. She extended her hand, hesitant to say goodbye to this woman she was quickly finding stunning and fascinating.

"Glad you got stuck with me," Jenny said with a sheepish smile.

Jenny looked down at Rya's hand then ignored it,

taking Rya in a warm hug. "It was nice getting to know you. I think Angie enjoyed it, too."

Rya paid attention to every tactile feeling, every scent and everything she saw as Jenny hugged her, so she could file it away as a memory to keep forever. "Well, um, safe travels home to Tucson."

Jenny gave her a winning smile and turned to the car, her hand on the handle before she turned back to Rya.

"Listen, would you like to get some coffee? I can run her back to the hotel…"

Startled to receive the invitation, it took Rya's mind a moment to catch up. Once it did, she was overjoyed.

"Absolutely."

⁂

"No, it was my parents that wanted me to be an actress," Jenny explained, sipping her caramel macchiato. "*The Bailers* was my first real project, other than commercials, some modeling gigs, things like that. I was only sixteen when I started on the show."

Rya smiled, leaning her cheek against her fist, her elbow resting on the small round table between them in the somewhat intimate dimness of the coffeehouse.

"Do you regret it? The acting that you did before you left Hollywood?"

Jenny shook her head.

"Hey, it paid for Stanford and my first house." She raised her mug in salute. "To wandering around WWII Germany for a season and a half."

Rya chuckled, raising her mug and clinking it against Jenny's.

"My favorite storyline of the entire series."

"So, what about you, Rya? Tell me about your life. What do you do for fun?"

"Well, there's the fly in the ointment," Rya began slowly. "I don't have fun. I work."

"Why? What do you do?"

"I manage *Burt's Diner*. Nothing special, but I put in tons of hours." She set her mug down and sat back in the booth seat. "To be honest, I stopped having fun seven years ago."

Jenny's delicate eyebrows drew together.

"Rya, you're a young woman. Why?"

"My partner and our ten-month-old were killed in a car accident," Rya said flatly.

Jenny stared at her for a long moment, only looking away when her brilliant eyes welled.

"I don't know what to say," she said softly.

Rya, touched by her emotion, said, "It's okay. You..." She cleared her throat. "The show helped me get through it."

Jenny tugged a napkin free from the dispenser at the center of their small table and dabbed at her eyes.

"Sorry." She took a moment before crumbling the napkin in her fist and giving a bright smile to Rya. "So, do you like animals?"

"Oh yeah, I love them," Rya said, unable to hold back. "Cats, in particular."

"Oh me too. Though..." Jenny said with a small sigh. "I lost my Munchkin last year."

"Oh, Jenny, I'm so sorry." Completely against her nature, she reached across the distance and briefly covered and squeezed Jenny's hand. "I have some kittens at my house right now. I inherited their mom, unbeknownst to me, pregnant."

"You do?" Jenny asked, eyes big and bright.

❧ ❧ ❧ ❧

They sat on the floor in Rya's laundry room, which currently doubled as the nursery. The mother cat, Libby, lay in the large box Rya had filled with towels, grooming one of her four kittens, the other three walking around like little drunken sailors.

"Oh my god," Jenny breathed. "They are so adorable."

"Yes. It's been a long time since I've had a kitten or a puppy." She grinned at her guest. "I forgot how much work they are."

"Oh," Jenny added, her voice dropping to an almost seductive level. "But the work has just begun."

Rya did her best to ignore how the tone affected her. "This is true." She cleared her throat in an attempt to clear her thoughts. "Those two are spoken for," she said, pointing to the two orange striped kittens. "So, now I'm trying to find homes for the other two before I get too attached and decide to keep them."

"Can I pick one up?" Jenny asked with childish glee.

Charmed, Rya nodded. "Of course."

With gentle hands, Jenny reached into the box and grabbed a mewling kitten, bringing the brown and black fur ball to her chest, nuzzling its soft head. "Hey, little fella."

Rya felt like an absolute pervert as she envied the kitten nestled against Jenny's gorgeous breasts. She brought a hand up and rubbed the back of her neck.

"You know," Jenny said softly, stroking the short length of the kitten that was falling asleep in her arms. "You may just talk me into it." She glanced up underneath her bangs at Rya.

"Into what?"

"Taking this little guy home."

Rya smiled. "What about his sister, little Oreo buns over there?" she said, indicating the black and white kitten, wobbling its way towards her mother.

Jenny grinned, gently replacing her furry bundle back into the box. "Seems to be nap time."

"Yes. It's almost two, their usual time to snooze." She grinned. "Well, that is, two, two fifteen, two thirty …"

Jenny laughed before turning back to the box. "Goodnight, adorable babies."

The two women pushed to their feet, Jenny stepping out into the short hallway where the doors to the laundry room, half-bath and garage were. Rya closed the laundry room door behind them so the kittens and their mother could get some rest, then joined Jenny in the dim hallway. Again, she felt their time was coming to an end, and she was incredibly sad because of it.

They stood nearly toe-to-toe in the narrow hallway, and Rya could feel her heart beginning to pound harder. As much as she desperately wanted to look away from Jenny's intense gaze, she couldn't. The actress took a step forward, and Rya took one backward, gasping in surprise as her back hit the wall next to the door that led to the garage. Jenny took another step, entering Rya's personal space, their breasts nearly touching.

"Rya," Jenny said softly, her gaze falling to take in Rya's lips before looking into her eyes.

Rya swallowed hard, nearly dizzy in the mixture

of arousal and confusion. "Yes?"

Jenny's hands rose up to rest on Rya's shoulders, slowly moving down until they rested on her hips. "I'm sorry, really I am," she said softly. "But, would it be incredibly inappropriate if I told you I've wanted to kiss you all day?"

Rya stopped breathing as her heart skipped a beat. Her gaze took in full, soft-looking lips. Her fingers itched to touch Jenny, but she felt paralyzed. "No," she managed.

At first touch, Jenny's lips were as soft as Rya had dreamed for years. She could never have imagined how her body would feel pressed against her. She could never have imagined the softness of her breasts or the warmth of her skin, the way she would smell and the way Jenny would touch her. Though her kiss was gentle and sensual, there was an underlying passion that Rya used to joke about with Shelby. She used to tell her she suspected that beneath the beautiful, sweet veneer, Jenny Jacobs was a little tiger, Rya remembered this as Jenny pinned her to the wall.

Within minutes the kiss deepened, getting hotter and wetter, much like Rya was. Left breathless, she looked into Jenny's eyes as they separated. With Jenny's hips still pressed into Rya's, she knew it was time. She'd grieved long enough.

Surprising even herself, she took Jenny by the hand and without a word led her upstairs to her bedroom.

Rya's eyes closed as she found herself standing next to the bed without a shirt and Jenny's mouth exploring her neck, a hand cupping her bra-clad breast. Her head fell back to give more access even as her hands blindly groped for the hem of Jenny's sweater. Finding it, she pushed the gorgeous redhead away just enough to lift the garment up and over her head before the two came back together in a fiery kiss, two sets of hands tugging on the remainder of each other's clothing.

Rya would have thought it amusing if she hadn't found herself breathless and flat on her back in her bed. She held Jenny on top of her, overwhelmed with the strength of her passion. Her mind began to short circuit, slowly losing detail by detail. She forgot it was Jenny Jacobs making love to her. She forgot it was this stunning woman making love to her. She forgot it was soft, silky hair trailing over her naked skin. She forgot her hard nipples teasing her own. She couldn't forget the tongue that slowly trailed through her drenched folds.

Rya's back arched as a long, languid moan escaped her throat and her legs fell fully open, exposing the depth of her arousal to Jenny's determined mouth. Her tongue was ruthless against Rya's rock hard clit, causing Rya to reach up behind her to grip the decorative bars of the headboard in an attempt to stay grounded as Jenny devoured her. It didn't take long before her throat was left raw from yelling out the intensity of her orgasm, the bed vibrating with the strength of her body's release.

Jenny kissed her way back up Rya's body, her hair a fiery curtain around them as they kissed, Rya's taste on Jenny's lips and tongue. She reached between them, tugging on rigid nipples as the kiss continued, Jenny moaning into her mouth. Wanting to touch her, Rya's hand reached down between their bodies, finding Jenny's drenched pussy.

Rya groaned deep in her throat in approval as her fingers found a hard, slick clit, rubbing it in tight circles. Jenny broke their kiss but remained where she was as her hips began to move, one knee hitching up on the mattress to offer more access to Rya's fingers.

"Come here," Rya murmured, indicating she wanted Jenny to straddle her. Once she did, two of Rya's fingers found their way inside Jenny's warmth, Jenny's head falling backward as she braced herself with hands resting on Rya's stomach.

"Fuck," Jenny whimpered as she moved her hips, slowly riding Rya's fingers.

Watching her fingers slowly disappear then reappear from inside Jenny was one of the most sensual things Rya had ever seen. As she looked down the length of her torso, she noticed the ruby red hardness of Jenny's clit and, her hand that had been cupping a breast made it's way down. She pressed her thumb against the pulsing flesh. With every movement of Jenny's hips, her clit rubbed against it.

Jenny gasped at the added pleasure, her hips beginning to move faster, her breathing increasing. Her eyes opened, and she met Rya's gaze, pure sex dripping from the stare in those turquoise eyes. Rya nearly came a second time from that look alone. Jenny's hips began to move nonstop. Her back arched as a keening sound began, and erupted into a loud cry as an inferno of wetness coated Rya's fingers. Rya moaned in sympathy, watching as Jenny's body convulsed once then a second time before it stilled, the gorgeous woman breathing hard.

Carefully removing her fingers, Rya sat up and wrapped her arms around Jenny, who eventually returned the embrace, her body still trembling. "Are you okay?" she asked softly.

Jenny let out a contented sigh, one of her hands

running up and down Rya's naked back as the fingers of her other hand combed through her messy hair. "Mm-hmm."

Her cheek resting against Jenny's upper chest, Rya let out a contented sigh, her eyes falling shut.

☙☙☙☙

Shelby's mouth hung open as she leaned on her elbow resting on the breakfast counter. "You're lying."

Rya, who stood on the business side of the breakfast bar making fresh coffee, shook her head. "No, I'm not."

"It's been a week. Why didn't you tell me about this?" the seated woman nearly shouted.

Rya smiled sadly. "I needed some time to process everything," she said softly.

"And, she was just gone, when you woke up?"

"Yup." Rya let out a heavy sigh as she leaned back against the counter, the coffee machine beginning to sputter to life.

"Wow. I have to admit. I have no idea what to say."

Rya glanced at her friend before looking into a memory that she would always cherish. "Nothing to say, Shel. It was one of the most beautiful days, and nights, of my life. Something I'll never forget."

"Yeah, no doubt. Wow." Shelby shook her head as she pushed to her feet. "I'm going to open up." She headed towards the door, the darkness of early morning beyond. "And," she added, glancing over her shoulder at her friend. "Nora Roberts will never be able to top this."

Rya chuckled, turning her back to the seating area of the diner to start brewing decaf. She heard a slight gasp, which concerned her. Worried something was wrong she turned, stopping short, eyes wide.

"Hi," Jenny said, walking up to the breakfast counter, a wide-eyed Shelby watching from the front door, which was slowly closing.

"Hi," Rya managed, her gaze leaving her friend to land firmly on the beautiful woman who had reached the counter. "Uh…coffee?"

Jenny grinned, taking a seat on one of the round stools, her elbows resting on the Formica countertop. "Well, I was thinking something more along the lines of dinner."

Rya eyed her, confused and unsure, even as her heart pounded in her chest. "I don't understand."

Jenny reached her arm across the counter, her palm up, her gaze meeting Rya's question. After a moment, Rya moved closer and placed her hand on Jenny's soft one.

"I'm sorry I disappeared this week. But, I had to head back to Arizona and tie up a few ends on the newest houses I'm flipping so I could get back here to spend some time with my new kittens…and you."

Rya felt her confusion turn to relief then deep affection, emotion prickling behind her eyes. "I see," she whispered, followed by a nervous laugh. "Okay. I think we can do that."

Kim Pritekel has been writing since she was nine-years-old, professionally since the age of twenty-four. She's a novelist, screenwriter, film director, and producer. Born and raised in the gorgeous state of Colorado, she enjoys all that entails. You can find her on Facebook.

The Oldest Convention Goer

By Karen Frost

She touched the ticket again. It was soft now, like downy cotton. She had folded and refolded it so many times that it was more like fabric than paper. It was crisscrossed by a hundred creases, like her palms, like her fingertips that stroked it thoughtlessly. She hadn't even noticed she'd done it. Her olive hands were permanently stained a deep brown from years in the sun, picking. What had they picked, season after season, all those years ago? It didn't matter anymore. Her hands shook, but not from nervousness. They did that now. She was an old woman, a clock slowly winding down.

She hadn't known if she was going to come. Until the last moment, she had considered not getting on the train. The ticket had been printed by her granddaughter and mailed to her because she didn't know how to use a computer. She could have said that she lost the ticket, could have sat at the station and watched the last car trundle past and then gone home. But she knew that she would go because she would have swum across all seven seas and climbed every mountain for her only granddaughter, the soul of her soul.

The girl had begged her to come, with her soft, hopeful voice, "Come, Amma, come, please, no one else will go. You must come. It's important."

She didn't understand what this was, this convention, but she could never say no to those pleading eyes, so much like those of her beloved mother. So she had boarded the train and come, clutching the ticket in her hand the whole time afraid that someone might snatch it away from her. Or perhaps she was scared that if she didn't cling hard enough, she would fling it away.

She slept fitfully on the train, her body jostling with every trestle the train passed over. Her body was too old to be comfortable now. When she dreamed, between flashes of the flat desert countryside, it was always the same thing, the black, almond eyes within a smiling face. Eyes that told her it was right for her to go, and she felt calm. She smiled in her sleep.

Her granddaughter met her on the platform, dancing with joy. She said, "Oh Amma, there are so many people here already. They're already in costume! I feel like Alice in Wonderland."

The old woman smiled wordlessly and got her small bag from the train.

She had made her granddaughter's sheriff's outfit herself, using photos the girl had mailed her. Her hands didn't shake when she sewed. The colors weren't right. She knew it when she saw the pictures on her granddaughter's phone in the hotel room. She was disappointed, but her granddaughter didn't mind. She twirled on her heel, showing off how the costume looked from all sides. Her hair was dyed red, and a smile like an angel stretched across her face. She posed, making her grandmother take pictures of her using her glittery cell phone for posting to...Instaface... Facegram? The old woman smiled gently and tapped the screen with her fingertip to take a picture as the girl had taught her.

"You'll see, Amma," her granddaughter said. "It will be magical. I've waited all year for this."

In long conversations on the phone, over the course of months, the girl had told her all about this sheriff. She was from a TV show with...demons? Vampires? The old woman had listened to the words as they flowed over her like water, but she didn't remember them. When she was older than the girl, she had watched soap operas on TV, but there were no vampires on them. People had not dressed like them, either. Still, she couldn't tell her granddaughter that she didn't need TV magic because she knew what real magic was. She didn't tell her about the beautiful almond eyes and the laughing, smiling mouth below them. She jealously guarded that remembered time when, after working long, hot hours in the field, they would lay down under the tree holding hands. Or the kiss they shared then.

Those were her secrets and her granddaughter didn't need to know them. To her granddaughter, she was just Amma, and that was all. She'd raised five children, staying up with them at night when they had fevers, taking them to the doctor when they broke arms, sewing holes in clothes, and preparing three meals a day. When all of her children had grown and left her, and her bones had ached, she had moved across the oceans to be near her daughter, who had moved to a new world, a new life. But hers had been a good enough life, and that was all the girl needed to know.

"Amma, this convention is about love," her granddaughter had explained, waving her hands as though they could tell a story that her mouth couldn't.

They were wild, passionate hands, full of

unexpressed words. She had her mother's hands, and her grandmother's before her.

"Yes, heart of my heart," the old woman had said.

"Amma, you're just saying that!" The girl protested.

"Okay," she replied patiently.

But she understood, the next day, what her granddaughter had meant when they walked among the vampires, the Valkyries, the sheriffs, the waitresses, and all the others who wore no costumes at all. The old woman could feel the love they had for each other, these strangers who had never met before and might never again. It was a love that lit the room like a thousand fires. A love they roared to the people on stage, and who gave it back in kind. The old woman marveled at the feeling, so unlike anything she had felt before.

"Do you see, Amma?" Her granddaughter asked, her face radiant as she basked in this nameless love.

"Yes, blood of my blood," she said. "I see."

Then the old woman, with her old eyes, saw the fields from her youth, where she had once held a girl's hand and promised to love her forever, no matter what. She saw the bitter unfairness of the world, a world that had ripped and torn at that love like a crazed, angry beast. She saw, in the room full of people swirling like schools of fish, all the futures that might have been for them, another time, another place. She didn't mind. She was too old to mind, now. The ghosts of her youth were not hungry. They did not hound her. They did not howl at her to remember them. And the world was not so unfair anymore. This convention was proof that the world had changed.

"This is new to me," she said to her granddaughter, gesturing to women holding hands and young women dressed in garish rainbow colors. "I am, perhaps, an antique here, yes?"

Her granddaughter laughed and hugged her, but gently. She giggled. "Then you're the antique Queen of the convention!"

The old woman couldn't explain to her granddaughter that she hadn't seen her first car until she was almost the same age as the girl was now. She couldn't tell her what it had been like to lie out under the stars, back when there were fewer cities in the world, and see so many stars that she wondered how they could all fit up in the sky. Back when two women, one with almond eyes, couldn't hold hands and love each other. A woman wearing a large black mustache and a cowboy hat walked past, and she watched her granddaughter rush to take a picture with the woman. She smiled gently. On the back of her neck, she felt the river breeze of her childhood tickle the short gray hairs there.

"Perhaps I'm too old to understand vampires, but I think I can understand love," she said quietly.

That night, her granddaughter lay with her head on the old woman's shoulder, running her long, delicate fingers over her grandmother's rough, calloused palms, tracing the deep lines etched in them. The old woman remembered how once a soothsayer told her the line by her thumb running to her wrist was her life line, while the line running horizontally along her palm was her heart line. Her heart line was strong but broken. Her life line was far too long.

"Amma," the girl said hesitantly. "Who is my real grandmother?"

"I am," the old woman said without hesitation, stroking the girl's short, tightly curled hair.

"Amma, be real. Look at us."

Her granddaughter held out her arm, and it was ebony black next to the old woman's wrinkled, tan skin. It was the same skin as her mother. The old woman looked into her granddaughter's black, almond eyes. A smiling ghost stared back, and she smiled in return.

"Soul of my soul," she said, pulling the girl into her chest tightly, "I am your grandmother."

She packed her small bag the next day and waved to her granddaughter from the small windows of the train, watching, as the girl became a doll, then a figurine as the car pulled away from the station. The girl had not asked again about her real grandmother, and that suited the old woman. Her secrets were hers. A young woman with a playful smile tugging at her lips looked at her from across the seat.

"How was the convention?" She asked.

Rubbing arthritis in her knobby fingers, the old woman sighed. "I didn't know I'd become so old. I don't understand the world anymore, but I can see that it makes them happy."

"I don't think you're too old to understand vampires," the young woman said, smiling broadly.

The old woman looked into the younger woman's dark, almond eyes and laughed, the sound of the wind rustling through dried leaves. She said, "I suppose no one is too old to understand vampires then."

The old woman paused, then said, "I know you would have liked it. It was, after all, about love."

Karen Frost is a freelance writer for AfterEllen and enjoys writing YA fiction in her free time. She lives in Washington, D.C. and her works can be found at https:// www.wattpad.com/user/DawnTreader2016.

The Two Queen Caper

By Julia Hosack

The note came three days ago. That's how we do things, Starr and I. We send notes. We've both left without saying goodbye so often that notes have become our thing. So now, here I am, standing in the middle of SFO, trying to catch a glimpse of the woman who occupies my dreams.

Starr and I have been friends for fifteen years, lovers even longer. We met on a grift. That's what we do. We con people. We pretend to be people we aren't, and we steal. Starr likes to steal things. She likes the short con, in and out in a day or two, a week tops. I play a different game. I like to become someone new, assume their life, play in their world for a while. The payout at the end is just another part of the thrill.

I stop to scan the crowd when I catch a flash of gold from the corner of my eye. I barely get my hand up to defend myself. A tall, lanky blonde tackles me. She wraps me in a bear hug, lifting me off the floor. Before I can react, her lips are on mine. Her words are reverberating in my head.

"Oh, God, how I miss you!"

I drop my bag before wrapping my arms around her neck, giving her a kiss that will make her toes curl.

"I miss you too, Starr. You have no idea how much I miss you."

"I think I do," she replies as she grabs my hand and leads me to her car while I contemplate, once again, how we got here. I wouldn't say it was love at first sight, more like lust. I had been working closely with a wannabe Aristotle. He was a lovely Greek gentleman with a fondness for British women and more money than he could spend. Things were going well until his older son returned home with Starr. She wanted his yacht. I just wanted her.

What we have is complicated. We've only spent days together, a stolen weekend, a tropical rendezvous. We don't work together, and we don't go after the same marks. Most importantly, we don't talk about the relationship. It's not ideal, not even close to healthy but it works. Mostly. I think about her all the time. I dream about her. When I wake next to someone else, I wish it were she. For now, I have her, at least for the weekend. I don't know what she has planned, but I can guess. My stomach clenches at the thought.

I slide into the passenger seat of Starr's rental and try to relax. New York to San Francisco is a long flight. Suddenly, I am attacked again. I turn my head in time to intercept the kiss, but she pins me to the door. With more privacy, Starr's hands are all over me, down my slacks and up my shirt. Her fingertips leave scorched spots where they land. I try to push her away.

"Starr! I can't breathe!"

"Sorry," she mumbles as she lets up a bit but her hands never stop. "It's been so long, Charlotte!"

"It's only been a couple of weeks."

"One week is too long. One day is too long. One minute…"

"I get it!" I say with a laugh. "Whose fault is that anyway?"

Starr gives me a puzzled look.

"What?" I ask.

"I don't know," she answers. "What are you saying? I thought this was what you, we, wanted? Missing each other desperately, the anticipation, the reunion?" She smiles slyly. "The sex."

"No. I mean yes. I mean, bloody Hell! I confused myself!"

Starr laughs.

"Got you all flustered, huh?" she teases.

I give her a suggestive look. "I think what I mean is that maybe you don't have to wait so long to write sometimes."

"Gotcha," she says as she leans close and kisses me again.

While Starr drives, I try to sort my thoughts, but my mind won't stop going over what she said. Is she right? Am I only in it for the thrill? Do I want something more from her? I honestly don't know what I would say if she ever asks.

She pulls up to the hotel. I'm confused. We usually avoid the big corporates, preferring places more intimate and less visible. She hands the keys to the valet and takes my arm as I get out of the car.

"Promise me you'll keep an open mind."

"What? "Why? What are you up to?"

My senses are assaulted by a whirlwind of color and sound, as she opens the door. The lobby is full of people of all ages, kids running around, some standing in groups, all in costume. Spandex, body make-up and strange looking weapons abound. I close my eyes. My fingers go to my temples. This is the last thing I expected, and it's shaken me.

"Oh, it's nothing," she says as she pulls me toward

the front of the hotel.

Starr pushes me gently from behind, letting the door close behind us. I turn toward her.

"What the bloody Hell is this?"

She laughs. "It's UniverseCon or StarCon or something like that."

I raise my eyebrows.

"GalaxyCon?"

"Yeah, that sounds right," she says. "How do you know that? This isn't exactly your scene."

I sigh. "Last year in Japan, I fleeced a super-collector out of a quarter-mil. He promised me he would bring me to a Comicon. I thought I had dodged that bullet."

She laughs. God, I love the sound of her laugh!

"Well, I'm glad you know something about it. Makes it easier to explain."

"What do you mean explain? Is this a job? You want us to work together?"

She laughs again. "I'm working. I thought you might like in on the fun."

I sigh again. "This is your idea of fun? Please tell me we have a room?"

"We have a suite. You want to see it?"

I slip my arm around her waist and pull her close. "I want to see you, without your clothes. Preferably on top of me."

"Good Lord, Charlotte," she whispers. "I want to see that too."

I try to keep up as she winds her way through the throngs of people. We duck to avoid being gored by a kid with long green horns.

"What the hell is that?" Starr asks as she pushes the girl out of her way.

Without even thinking the words "Space Pop" tumble out of my mouth. Starr turns and stares as I quickly cover my mouth with my hand, my eyes wide. Her mouth opens to ask the question, and I quickly shake my head.

"I don't know," I say with horror in my voice. "It just came out. Damn it Taki-san!" I say, shaking my head as if to dislodge something. "Get out of my head!" More laughter. I'm glad Starr is having fun here.

We make it to her room without further incident. It's obvious Starr has been here. Dirty clothes litter the floor. My nose wrinkles and she sticks her tongue out at me. As she heads toward the bathroom, she calls over her shoulder, "get used to it!" I'm left wondering again. What exactly is she trying to tell me?

She comes back, much more subdued. She sits softly next to me.

"How're you doing, Char?"

I give a puzzled look, not sure if she's talking about the moment or my life. She looks as if she might say something then changes her mind.

"You want to go out? Have something brought up?"

I shrug.

"You should eat something. Wine?"

I shake my head. The last thing I need right now is something clouding my mind. Just her being near is intoxicating enough. She's said some strange things today. Does she finally want something more from me? Do I from her? The whole thing is making my head hurt. Fortunately, Starr has a way of stopping me from thinking for a while.

She begins to unbutton my blouse, her fingers lingering every time they find flesh. I can hear myself softly moan as she slides the fabric over my shoulders, unhooking my bra.

"I think about this all the time," she whispers as her soft lips meet mine. She pushes me back and hovers over me, staring, before lowering herself to me. I moan again as she takes a nipple into her mouth, teasing with her tongue and teeth until it is painfully erect before moving to the other. Her hands are down my slacks now, caressing me through my panties. I know she can feel how much I want her. I lift my hips for her to slide them off. Her fingers walk their way up the inside of my thigh, her lips not far behind. I'm squirming beyond control while she takes her time. I'm ready to beg, by the time she finally touches me.

"God, Starr! That feels good!"

"Mmm, I hope so," she hums as she slides two fingers deep inside. My fingers are twisted in her hair, holding her close as she continues to tease me with light touches, a slow and steady rhythm.

"Starr. Please," I am begging now, desperate for her to put me out of this delicious misery. She increases her speed, sucking on my clit until I finally let go amidst a full body contraction. She smiles at me as I ride out the aftershocks.

"You are beautiful," she says softly. "I love watching you like that, love being the one that makes you feel so good."

She rises, taking her clothes off and turning out the lights. She climbs in behind me, wrapping her arms tight around my still limp body.

"Tell me about Taki-san?"

"What? Why? He was just a mark. Why are you even thinking about this right now?"

"I don't know." She shrugs. "Did you sleep with

him?"

"We don't do this, Starr, remember? We don't talk about work…or anything else. Why now? What do you want me to say?"

"I don't know," she repeats. "I just can't stand the idea of other people touching you. Not like I do."

"I didn't sleep with him. Okay?"

"Okay."

She nuzzles her face into my hair with a contented sigh.

"Starr?"

"Yeah?"

"No one touches me the way you do."

"Thanks, Charlotte."

"You're welcome."

❧❧❧❧

Starr is in no hurry to talk about the job. We have a leisurely breakfast while we watch the con-goers mingle in the lobby. It amuses me how people of all ages and fandoms mix as if this were something they did every day. As a student of human nature, I find it fascinating. As a woman of sophistication, I am slightly horrified to be present.

Dishes cleared, Starr finally decides to talk business. She pulls out her iPad and starts flipping through photos. Finding the one she's looking for, she sets the tablet on the table, sliding it toward me. I look down at a picture of what appears to be a jeweled scepter. I push the iPad to her.

"Pretty. What is it?"

"Besides the obvious you mean?" she asks with a smile.

"Yeah, you're a comic genius," I tell her. "What's

its story?"

"Well," she starts, "it belongs to an inconsequential princess from a little principality in Europe. Too much time and money on her hands."

I rub my hands together. "Ooh, I do like stealing from the rich!"

She laughs again. "Well, then, you'll love this job because this girl is quite wealthy and not pleasant. She's a big fan of Alice in Wonderland, likes to think of herself as the Red Queen, off with her head, and all that. She had this made as part of her cosplay."

"Interesting. The Red Queen huh? I love a bad girl. Is it real?"

She shrugs. "I don't know. Probably. I was hired to get it. I get paid whether it's real or not."

Starr has always done this kind of contract work. She likes the challenge of planning the heist, thinking on her feet, and the guaranteed payday. I work more for the love of the game, the more challenging the grift, the better.

"Okay," I say, "I'm assuming that this is not just a straight up lift then?"

She shakes her head. "It's going to be a bit more complicated than that, a swap. She can't know that it's gone. Part of the deal."

"So, we break into her room? I still don't see why you need me for this?"

"I need you because we're going to take it out of her hand, on stage, in front of a room full of people."

I raise my eyebrows at that.

"Really? You couldn't handle an easy lift and drop by yourself?"

She shakes her head again. "No. Well maybe, but it'll go better with two grifters. Besides, I wanted to see you. Good enough?"

I smile. "Good enough. What's the plan?"

❧❧❧❧

We go for a long walk along Fisherman's Wharf before grabbing a late lunch. I watch as she fiddles with the stem of her wine glass.

"Do you want to talk about it?"

"What?"

"What's bothering you, Starr? What is this really about?"

She shrugs. "I don't know. Have you ever thought about getting out of the game?"

"Not really. I figure I'll be dead or in prison long before I have to make that decision."

"Well, that's a cheery thought," she says wryly.

"Realistic, though. Is that what you're wanting? To get out?"

"It's crossed my mind. I get so tired of always running. Haven't you ever thought about settling down? About having a family? Being with someone you love?"

"I hope that someone you're thinking about isn't me."

I am horrified by the words as they come out of my mouth, but it's too late to take them back. Her eyes turn cold, and she forces a smile.

"No, of course not. It was just a thought."

Our food arrives, and we eat in silence, my harsh words hanging between us like a curtain.

Back in the room, Starr is full of nervous energy.

"Are you always like this before a job?" I ask.

"I don't know, Charlotte. I don't like the waiting. There's something else. Something doesn't feel right. I can't put my finger on what it is."

"Too many moving parts?" I suggest.

She shrugs. "I don't know. I've got it all worked out. It should go as planned."

"Nothing goes as planned," I tell her, "you know that. But it's all good. You've got it covered. We've got this."

She smiles. "You're right. We've got this."

I nod. "Now come here and try to relax." I pat the bed next to me.

She comes to me, and I rest my hand on her thigh.

"You want me to rub your shoulders?" I ask. She shakes her head.

"You want me to rub something else?"

I get off the bed and drop to my knees in front of her, wrapping my hands around her and pulling her to the edge of the bed.

"You need to learn to relax," I tell her as I push her skirt up. She puts her hands in my hair and murmurs, "mmm, this might work…"

I smile as I begin to taste my way up the inside of her thigh, kissing and caressing every new bit of skin. She sighs as she tangles her fingers tighter in my hair. I start playing with her clit, slowly circling, dipping inside to gather her wetness. When she finally feels my hot mouth on her, she groans and falls back on to her hands, head hanging back. I move slowly and rhythmically, my palms kneading her thighs where they meet her body, sucking and nibbling in all the places I know she likes. When she begins to tense, I stop, just long enough for her to start squirming. She tries to pull me closer, begging for a finish. With a smile, I give her what she wants, and she collapses backward onto the bed. Slowly, I get up and crawl on top of her. She wraps her arms around me, and whispers, "Oh my God, Char!

You can rub me there any time you want."

She rolls me to her side, her arms still wrapped tight around me. I can feel her breathing slowly as she falls asleep. I lie with her, feeling her warm breath on my cheek, thinking about what it would be like to have her anytime I want.

I wake to Starr shoving a duffel bag into my hand, and moving me toward the bathroom while she starts to fiddle with her hair. I open the bag and pull out a pair of fishnets and a bright red corset.

I call out to her, "Starr! You cannot be serious!"

"You'll be the hottest Red Queen ever," she yells back.

"I may be hot, but I sure won't be warm," I mutter.

"What?"

"Nothing."

I call her in to help me tie the corset. She hasn't gotten much farther with her cosplay than a messy braid and glitter make up. She laces up the ribbons and pulls the corset tight, squeezing the breath out of me. I look down and realize that's not the only thing that's being squeezed out.

"Umm, Starr…"

She turns me around. "Oh my God," she says under her breath as she takes in the thigh-high fishnets and corset with my breasts popping out of the top. Her eyes go down to my bosom, and she stares.

"Starr. Starr!"

"Mmm, Charlotte…"

"Starr! My eyes are up here," I say gesturing with my hands. Her eyes don't move.

"I know."

I put my hand under her chin and lift her face up, so her eyes meet mine.

"You have a problem!"

"I know," she says with a smile. "But it's a good problem to have."

I roll my eyes. "I remember the first night we met," I tell her playfully. "You looked down the front of my dress then too."

She looks surprised. "You saw that?"

"Of course I saw that. I was too busy checking you out to say anything."

"That's not exactly how I remember it," she says with a smile.

"Really? Are you sure?" I ask her suggestively as I take a chance with the physics of garment design and push my breasts into her. I can see her trying to fight the urge to look down again. Her fingers are twitching, and I can only imagine what she's thinking.

"It's okay, Starr, just a peek, and no touching. You're just going to have to wait."

I let her get another good look then turn her around and push her out of the bathroom.

The rest of the outfit consists of a gorgeous overcoat and a very short black skirt. The velvet coat is blood red and trimmed in black and gold. The collar stands up almost past my head. The only buttons are at the bottom giving everyone a full view of my chest. The skirt skims the top of my stockings, and bright red stiletto boots complete the outfit. I am playing with different hairstyles when Starr comes up behind me.

"Here, let me help you with that," she says as she piles my dark hair to the top of my head and secures it with a gold tiara. She pulls tendrils down to frame my face and declares me perfect.

I turn around to see what she is wearing, and I am stunned. Her dress is light blue and shimmery.

The translucent fabric is stretched tight across her, not hiding any part of her beautiful curves. Her shoulders are bare and sparkle with pale blue glitter. I try to talk, but my mouth is dry.

"You like?" she asks.

I nod.

"A lot?"

I nod again and reach out, touching her ribs, letting my hand slide down the slick fabric to her hip. She turns away with a laugh.

"No touching, remember?" My knees feel weak, and I have to lean against the counter for a few seconds before I follow her out.

From another bag, she pulls a gold scepter. I take it from her and examine it. It's an expensive and perfect forgery. The mark shouldn't notice the switch unless she examines it carefully. I swing it around over my head.

"Off with her head!"

Starr laughs. "Perfect!"

We head down to the convention floor and walk arm in arm through the crowds. I'd like to think it's me turning heads, but I am pretty sure it's The Ice Queen gliding along next to me who is generating the stares and whispers. Starr checks the time. And we move to the ballroom for the cosplay contest. As we take the stage, Starr kisses me and wishes me luck. I position myself near the Red Queen. Starr is behind me. The fake scepter is in my hand. All I need is a distraction, which is conveniently provided by the ridiculous boots Starr put me in. I snag my heel on the carpet and fall forward into the mark, knocking her down and landing on top of her. While we scramble to regain some of our dignity, I make the switch, sliding the real scepter behind me where Starr can retrieve it. The mark grabs the fake from my hand, giving me a hateful look before moving to the other side of the stage. All I want to do is disappear, but someone pushes me to the front for my moment of fame. I take my winner's handshake with a smile then leave the room as quickly as the crowd will let me.

I meet Starr back in the suite. She's already ordered champagne and strawberries to celebrate our victory. The scepter is on the bed, and I examine it while I drink my wine. She watches me without comment.

"This thing is probably worth a fortune. It's too bad you already have a buyer. I wouldn't mind having something like this around." She raises her eyebrows.

I laugh. "I am a member of the aristocracy after all." I know she doesn't believe me, but we both have our secrets.

Starr finishes her glass and comes to me, taking the scepter and dropping it to the floor. She pulls me to standing and makes a point to look down my front.

"You promised I could touch."

"I did, did I? Help me get out of this thing then."

She softly runs her fingers across the top of my breasts then reaches around to loosen the ribbon on my corset. She lets it fall to the floor as her hands travel up my back. The whole time her eyes never leave my chest.

Fair is fair, and I put my hands where her dress is pulled tight across her hips. I can't help but run my hands up her sides. Without my coat and corset, I'm wearing nothing but my stockings and boots. I can tell it's driving Starr a little crazy. I pull her close, enjoying the way her second skin feels against mine. She kisses me while I gently rub myself against her.

We turn together, and she lowers me to the bed. She's on her knees now, between my feet as she pulls my boots off. She slowly rolls the stockings down, one at a time, following their trail with gentle kisses down my leg. Her fingers deliberately trace back up as she pulls herself onto me, lowering her mouth to my breast. I catch my breath as her tongue begins to explore.

I am still fascinated with the warm, slick fabric of her dress, running my hands up and down her firm body. She sinks a knee between my legs, and I slide onto it, holding tight.

"You like the dress?" she asks as she pushes harder.

"Yeah," I say, my voice hoarse. "I like the dress."

I find the zipper, and I slowly work it down.

"I like this too," I say as I caress her bare skin.

"Do you want me to take it off?" she asks again, moving her knee against me.

I close my eyes. "Not yet," I croak. It gets harder to catch my breath. Starr slowly pulls her knee away as she leans down to kiss me.

"Tease!"

"Patience," she whispers as she begins to work her way down my body with her lips and her tongue. I squirm underneath her, but she won't let me hurry. She slides her fingers inside of me, and I hear myself cry out. We move in a steady rhythm, my hips rising to meet her on every thrust. Just as I'm reaching my peak, she slows.

"Bloody Hell, Starr!"

"Be careful, Love." She laughs. "Your British is showing."

With a grin, she begins to move again, rubbing hard against me until I come with another cry.

I lie still, enjoying the feeling of Starr's weight

on top of me. She rolls away to get more champagne. When she returns, her dress is gone. I give her an approving look as she hands me the wine with a smirk. I empty the glass and drop it to the floor.

"You are so beautiful, Starr."

Her face is very close to mine. I'm staring, lost in her sparkling blue eyes when she decides to speak.

"Charlotte. You are...I..." She pauses, choosing her next words carefully. "I miss you when we're not together."

I hear her, but it's her eyes that are speaking the truth. I can see what she wants to say. I can also see the flash of uncertainty, of fear. Her words would have been against the rules. My rules. Her rules. Keep it casual. No commitments. No emotions. We've said the L-word before but only in play. To say it now, that would be contrary to everything we say we want. I fight back a tear. I would have told her that I love her, too. How I've always loved her. How I think I always will. Instead, I whisper, "I miss you too, Starr."

We share a kiss that feels like all the words we can't say. She settles in next to me, our noses almost touching. We make love slowly this time, deliberately, letting our fingers trace shapes and lines, find familiar places. Everything is perfect now. I have nothing I want to say. I just want to be. Want Starr to be. To make this moment last forever. She pulls me close, and we come together, and it is exquisite.

Starr falls asleep with her arms around me, my head on her shoulder. I lie awake thinking about words we didn't say, what it would mean if we did. This relationship, this obsession, could it last in real life? This isn't real. We aren't real. We're a fantasy, a dress up game like the kids downstairs play. It's satisfying and heartbreaking at the same time. I just don't know if I want to change, or if I could. Starr rolls into me, throwing her leg over mine with a deep sigh. I let her touch soothe me and finally drift off to sleep.

When I wake in the morning, Starr is gone. I raise my fist and let it fall hard onto the bed next to me. Leaving abruptly, no goodbye, no explanation, it's our thing, but it still hurts every time. I get out of bed, rubbing my temples where they ache from too much champagne. I scan the room, knowing it will be here somewhere. I find her note stuck to the bathroom mirror.

"Have biz. Back soon."

I smile, the sick, lonely feeling in my stomach subsiding.

When Starr returns, I am wrapped in a robe, propped up by pillows on the bed, flipping through a magazine full of tourist propaganda. She comes flying in with a big smile. She drops a thick envelope onto the bed next to me.

"It's done," she says.

I pick up the envelope and ruffle through the stack of $100 bills.

"Nice. Well done."

"We should celebrate!" she says. Before I can respond, the phone in her pocket rings.

She listens carefully, and I watch her face change from pleased to concerned to angry.

"Okay, thanks," she tells the person on the end of the line. She presses the button to hang up her phone, stares at it for a second then turns and throws it hard against the wall.

"Starr?"

She turns back to me, and I can see the fire in her

68

eyes.

"Get dressed, Char! We need to go! Now!"

I hurry to get dressed while she quickly shoves her things into her bag.

"What is going on?" I demand.

She stops and looks at me.

"My fence just turned up dead."

"What does that mean?"

"It means it was a setup."

"I don't understand, to get to you? What are you into?"

"It was a long time ago," she says quietly. "I took something I shouldn't have. I was hoping it would go away, but it's not ever going to go away. So now I need to go away."

"What? Where? Give me time to pack my things."

"Alone. I can't put you in any more danger than I already have. I'll contact you when I can if I can. Just remember, Charlotte, remember I..."

"No!" I stop her. "Not now. Not like this. Please? Not like this?"

She nods.

"Let me get my stuff, and then I'll help you figure this out."

She nods again.

When I return from the bedroom, Starr is gone. I frantically search, but there's nothing to be found. For the first time, she didn't leave a note.

Julia Hosack is an avid fanfiction writer, artist, and comicon vendor as well as retired Special Education PE teacher. She is married and lives with her two kids and seven furries in Southwest Washington. This is her first original work.

Present and Future Tense

By eternaleponine

By midmorning, Taylor had to admit that maybe Brenn had been right.

Her day started with a pillow to the face launched by her roommate and accompanied by the announcement that Taylor needed to get up because they were leaving in half an hour, despite the fact that Taylor was sure she had not agreed to go anywhere. She'd expected to spend this weekend the same way she'd spent every weekend for the last several months, in her apartment, creating artwork that no one would ever see and feeling sorry for herself.

"We're going to the con," Brenn said. "You need to get dressed. Wear something nerdy."

Taylor sat up, pushing her hair out of her face. "I thought you were going with—"

"Don't even say his name," Brenn replied, her lip curling. "I bought the tickets, so I get to go with whoever I want, and I want to go with you. Now get up."

"It's not my thing," Taylor said, even though she knew it wouldn't fly. She tried again saying, "I don't want to drag you down."

"If you don't want to drag me down, don't," Brenn said as if it were that simple. "It's not going to kill you to leave the house and interact with a subsection of the human race. You might even decide you like it and consider rejoining."

Taylor had serious doubts.

Now she was here, and it wasn't as bad as she'd expected it to be. Seeing all of the costumes and wandering the aisles of vendors was kind of cool, even if she didn't recognize half of the fandoms. She felt a pang as she wandered down Artists' Alley, but she tried not to let the feeling take root. She'd made her choice, and she had to believe that it was the right one, not just for herself but everyone else.

Brenn sidled up next to her and bumped Taylor with her shoulder. "I'm going to a panel," she said. "'Science or Science Fiction?' It seems like it might be pretty cool. Want to come?"

Taylor shook her head. "Have fun. Don't get yourself kicked out correcting the panelists if the science wrong."

Brenn grinned. "Yeah, no promises on that one. I'll find you after."

"See you." She kept wandering, smiling at people who smiled at her, trying to act as if she belonged here. Six months ago, she would have. Six months ago, she would have been right in the thick of things.

Six months ago, she was a different person.

"Hey," someone said, and she turned to find a girl who looked to be her age, maybe a little younger, standing just a little too close for comfort. "I love your shirt," the girl said. "Infected319, right?"

Taylor's heart slammed against her ribcage, and she stumbled back half a step. It took her a second to realize that the girl was referring to the artist, not to her specifically, even though they were one and the same.

"I have a different one," the girl said. "I didn't wear it though. After what happened on the show, and then with all the drama, I just…" She shrugged.

"Yeah," Taylor said, forcing a smile, then glanced down at the watch that she wore that no longer worked. This girl wouldn't know that. "Sorry, I have to go meet someone." She darted off before the girl could say anything else, and rushed out of the exhibition hall and away from everyone. She crashed through the door of the nearest restroom, ducked into a stall and collapsed onto the seat, putting her head in her hands, her palms pressing into her eyes until she saw stars.

Coming here was a mistake. At least wearing this shirt was. When Brenn handed it to her, she should have given it right back and found something else. Sure, she was proud of the art she'd created, had gained a significant following because of it, but when you were trying to disappear from fandom, going to a con as a walking billboard for yourself was probably a bad idea.

She heard the door open and the sound of the sink turning on. She stayed where she was until it started to feel awkward like she was creeping on this woman who didn't even know she was there. Still, she hesitated, listening for the sound of the door and then wondering if maybe somehow she'd missed it because she didn't hear anything else. She stood up, and the toilet automatically flushed as she pulled open the stall door.

"Oh!" The girl at the mirror turned around quickly. "I didn't realize—shit!"

"What?" Taylor asked. "What's wrong?"

"I dropped my contact," the girl said.

"Shit," Taylor agreed and then set about looking for it because it was her fault that she'd dropped it in the first place. After a few seconds, she found it stuck to the counter and picked it up gingerly, extending her finger to transfer it to the girl's hand. "I hope you have lens solution."

"I do," the girl said, fumbling through her makeup case and pulling it out, her forehead furrowing as she concentrated on cleaning off the lens before quickly popping it into her eye and reaching for the other one. "Thank you."

"You're welcome," Taylor said, feeling awkward just standing there watching her, but walking away at this point would be...rude? "Great costume, by the way," she added, trying to salvage the situation.

"Costume?" The girl looked down at herself and turned to look at Taylor. Her head cocked slightly to one side. It was only then that Taylor realized who was standing a few feet away.

At the same time, the girl seemed to take in Taylor's shirt, and her mouth twitched, although her expression stayed carefully neutral.

Oh shit.

It wasn't a fellow fan in costume. This wasn't someone pretending to be Allie from *The Infected*. This was Allie, or more accurately, Alexandria Woods, who played Allie. Standing right in front of her, staring at her shirt with the fanart version of herself.

This was a disaster.

How had she not known that she was one of the guests at the con? Why had Brenn not warned her?

But then the other girl's expression slid into a smile, her green eyes lighting up as her lips curved upward. "I guess the secret's out now," she said. "If it wasn't for all of the dirt and fake blood, I could wear my clothes on set, and no one would know the difference."

"Do you ever get to be clean?" Taylor joked.

Alexandria seemed to consider this for a moment.

"I think I took a shower once back in season two," she said.

"And you ended up covered in grease like two scenes later," Taylor pointed out.

"I guess that's your answer then," she said. She held out her hand. "I'm Alexandria 'Andi' Woods, by the way."

I know, Taylor thought. From the flush that rose in Andi's cheeks, it seemed she had realized how ridiculous the introduction was. "Taylor," she said, taking her hand and shaking it. "Nice to meet you."

"You too," Andi said. "I like your shirt."

"Thanks," Taylor said, fighting the urge to cross her arms over her chest. "If I'd known I was going to meet you I probably would have chosen a different one."

"Why?" Andi asked. Taylor opened her mouth, and then closed it again. She didn't have an answer that she thought Andi would understand. Andi smiled again, a gentle smile like she thought Taylor needed reassurance. Maybe she did, but Taylor didn't want to be that person, that awkward, tongue-tied fan.

"I think it's amazing, the passion that people have, the creativity. I honestly had no idea that it would—could—be like that. I had no idea what I was getting into when I first got cast for the show. I don't think anyone did. It was just, 'Okay, I've got a job, the character is cool, the story looks pretty interesting, let's see where it goes.' And then the fans got hold of it, and it just took on this whole other life, this whole other dimension, and I was... blown away. You know?"

Taylor nodded. "Yeah. It can be pretty intense." *To say the least,* she thought.

Something flickered in Andi's eyes, and she

looked away, glancing at herself in the mirror and tucking back a stray strand of hair. Taylor knew that the polite thing to do would be to excuse herself, leave Andi alone to finish getting ready, but then Andi caught her eye in the mirror and the corner of her mouth quirked up.

"Is it just me, or is there suddenly a giant elephant in the room?" she asked, obviously trying to break the tension that hung between them.

"Why did the elephant paint its toenails red?" Taylor asked, wincing inwardly at the lameness of the joke, but it was the first thing that popped into her head.

"I don't know," Andi said. "Why?"

"So it could hide in the strawberry patch."

Andi laughed, a soft, uncertain chuckle, and Taylor forced a smile in return. It didn't make things better, but what could they do or say? They both knew they were on opposite sides of an invisible but very real line. Even if Andi wanted to say something about it, Taylor doubted she was allowed. Even though this conversation was strictly off the record, and even though she wasn't the kind of person who would post things all over the internet, Andi didn't know that, didn't know her. She couldn't take that sort of chance. Andi started to put things back into her makeup bag. Before Taylor could think of a polite way to cut and run, the door opened.

"Andi, it's time to go," someone said. "Panel's in ten."

She seemed to deflate a little, then pulled herself back up. It was like a mask slipped into place, a pleasantly neutral mask to face the world, and fandom. "I've gotta go," she said, "but maybe I'll see you there? Or later?"

"Maybe," Taylor said, but she doubted it. Their respective roles didn't change after a few minutes of awkward conversation in which the silence had said far more than the words they'd exchanged.

And seriously, how much could Andi possibly want to see Taylor?

But as Andi reached for the bathroom door, which her handler was still holding open, she turned back and smiled again, a smile that sent a flurry of butterflies through Taylor's stomach. "I hope so," she said.

And then she was gone.

❧❧❧❧

Taylor went to the panel for *The Infected* but sat near the back to have a clear route to the exit. She barely heard what the moderator asked the cast members. She tuned out everyone except Andi. When they opened the session for fan questions, Taylor held her breath, afraid that Andi might be put on the spot, forced to defend a decision that hadn't been hers to make or to find some way to dodge it.

Do you ever regret it?

The question echoed through Taylor's head as she watched her sitting up there, looking completely at ease like she was born for this.

Do you ever wish you could just be Andi again, and not Allie, not a symbol, a figurehead for fans to build a cause behind?

If you could go back and do it all over again, would you?

Impossible questions with equally impossible answers...

But it gave Taylor an idea.

⁂

Brenn seemed surprised when Taylor said she wanted to go back to the con with her the next day. "Socializing two days in a row?" Eyebrows raised and arms crossed, she'd looked Taylor up and down. "Who are you and what did you do with my friend?" She laughed, but Taylor wasn't sure she was joking.

Taylor tucked the big cardboard envelope she carried carefully under her arm and checked the convention app for the schedule. She hadn't thought to check ahead of time whether Andi was going to be there both days. Her stomach clenched as she scrolled through and didn't find her name. Finally, it popped up, and the rush of relief left her feeling a little shaky.

"You okay?" Brenn asked.

Taylor nodded. "Yeah," she said. "Fine. I just have to go see somebody about something."

Brenn's eyebrows went up. "How specific," she said dryly. "You have fun with that."

"I will," Taylor said. She approached the booth to buy tickets for autographs from the guests, praying that they wouldn't be sold out. When she approached, the person manning the booth smiled and said she was in luck, there were still a few more, and wasn't the show awesome? Taylor nodded and thanked them when they handed her the ticket that would get her another chance to talk to Andi, even if it was only for a minute or two, with someone watching over their shoulders the entire time.

She tried to distract herself because the signing wasn't for hours yet, but she found it impossible to focus on anything, and eventually, she just found a corner to sit and sketch for a while, hoping that the familiar feeling of pencil on paper would soothe her frayed nerves. It was hard to capture anyone in detail because as soon as she started to sketch, the person who'd caught her eye disappeared into the crowd again.

After what felt like forever she got up and went to find the line, not wanting to risk being at the end of the queue and running out of time before she got to see Andi. She tried to block out the chattering of the people around her, existing in her little bubble as the line crawled forward. After what felt like an eternity, she reached the front of the line and approached the table holding the envelope in front of her like a shield.

Andi had turned to say something to the man standing behind her, and when she turned back her brilliant green eyes went wide, the corners crinkling as she smiled and said, "We meet again."

Taylor held out the envelope. "This is for you," she said.

"Thank you," Andi said automatically, as she pulled the paper out from inside the envelope.

Taylor had been up most of the night creating the image, which showed Allie bound in chains she was attempting to break free of, as hands, some of them the infected, some not reached for her and tried to grab her and pull her down.

"Oh," she said softly. "This is..." She looked up at Taylor, and for a second Taylor thought she saw the faintest shimmer of tears in her eyes. "You made this?" Taylor nodded. "It's amazing," she said. "I don't even know what to say."

"I'm glad you like it," Taylor said.

"I love it," Andi said. She looked down at it again, the tips of her fingers tracing the edge of the paper.

The silence hung there between them as Andi's

focus stayed on the picture as if she was trying to memorize every detail. Taylor finally cleared her throat, and Andi's head snapped up like she'd forgotten she wasn't alone.

"I hope you have a good rest of the con," Taylor said. She turned to walk away to let the next person have their chance, but Andi reached out, rising half out of her seat to catch Taylor's wrist.

Taylor looked down, and then back at Andi, who immediately released her grip, her cheeks flooding with color. "I'm sorry," she said. "Did you want...?" She gestured vaguely at the pictures on the table next to her.

"No," Taylor said. "I just wanted to give you the picture."

"Oh." Andi sat back down. "You have a good rest of the con too." Her smile had faded completely, and she looked confused or maybe disappointed. But why would she be disappointed?

Taylor turned again because now she was being motioned to move along by someone in a neon staff shirt.

"Wait." Andi's voice stopped her, made her turn and go back to the table as Andi beckoned her closer. "Meet me after," she said. "Outside the green room area." Taylor opened her mouth, but before anything came out, Andi added, "Please."

It was the magic word. Taylor nodded, and then gave in to the person responsible for herding fans out of the signing area.

She found the green room, the area where guests were allowed and fans were not, and stayed just far enough away so she wouldn't draw attention to herself from security. She didn't know why Andi had asked her to meet here, and she was reasonably sure she was going to end up looking like an idiot, waiting for someone who was never going to show up, but she stayed anyway.

"Hey."

She looked up from her sketchbook, and her heart thumped harder when she found herself locked in Andi's gaze. "Hey." She tucked her pencil into the coil at the top, and stuffed the pad into her bag, pushing herself up to a standing position while subtly trying to adjust her clothing back into place.

They eyed each other for a long moment, Taylor waiting for an explanation as to why Andi had asked her here, and Andi just watching her, studying her as intently as she'd studied the picture. "Your shirt yesterday," she said. "That was yours, wasn't it? The art?"

Taylor nodded.

"I looked it up last night," Andi said.

Please tell me you didn't Google 'The Infected fanart,' Taylor thought. *Please tell me you didn't make that mistake.* But how else would she have found it? It wasn't like she'd taken a picture of the shirt that she could then use to reverse image search. She was suddenly gladder than ever that anything she'd been inspired to draw that would have rated an NSFW tag had remained safely in her sketchbook.

"I found the other stuff you've done, but I didn't see this one." Andi held up the envelope with Taylor's art in it.

"I just made that one last night," Taylor said. "For you."

"You did this all in one night?" Andi shook her head. "I'm even more impressed."

"It's not a big deal," Taylor said. "It's pretty easy

when you're inspired." She didn't say that it had been a while since she'd felt that kind of inspiration.

"Andi!" They both turned to look at the man calling to her. "It's time to go."

She grimaced, looking at Taylor like she was disappointed to cut their conversation short. She glanced back at the man who was watching them, not so patiently waiting, then blurted, "Come with me."

Taylor blinked. "What? Where?"

"Just to the airport," Andi said. "I'll make sure you get a ride back, here or home or wherever you need to go."

Taylor started to shake her head and stopped herself. She didn't know what was happening here, why Andi was inviting her along on her ride to the airport. It didn't make sense, but if she said no, she would regret it. Sometimes you only got one shot, and even if you didn't know what you were shooting at, you still needed to take it. "Let me just text my friend," she said, already typing out a message to Brenn to let her know she was going to get a ride home on her own.

In the car, they were quiet, side by side and not even looking at each other until they were on the highway. Andi's eyes flicked to their driver before coming back to Taylor. "After I found your art, I looked you up," she said.

Oh. "I'm sorry," Taylor said.

"Don't be," Andi said. "I just..." She nudged the corner of the envelope at her feet. "This isn't just about Allie. Is it?" Taylor didn't answer. She didn't need to. Silence settled around them again, not tense but heavy. The elephant was back in the room. Minutes passed. "We're not so different, you and I," Andi said.

Taylor looked at her, and now there was tension,

like a rubber band that had been stretched as far as it could go and was trying to return to its original shape, to equilibrium.

Was that even possible? Even if they were in some ways the same, weren't they like two magnets with the same polarity, pushing against insurmountable forces to try and find a way to meet in the middle?

We're not magnets, Taylor thought. *We're people. We're just two girls.*

The car stopped, and the rubber band snapped, sending them back to their neutral corners. "Sorry," the driver said. "Just some traffic. Shouldn't hold us up too much."

When the car started moving again, Andi looked over at Taylor. "The things that people said to you, the way that they turned on you...it wasn't fair."

Taylor shrugged. *Didn't anyone ever tell you that life isn't fair?* "People were hurt by what happened. They were angry. Maybe some people were looking for ways to misinterpret things, looking for reasons to lash out at someone or provoke a reaction. I was an easy target, and I could handle it." *Right up until I couldn't.*

Right up until she walked away.

Andi stared down at her hands. "Sometimes the things you want to say, the things you should say, and the things that you can say, get all tangled up. Sometimes, no matter how much you don't want to, you have to speak from your head and not your heart." She looked over at Taylor as if seeking approval, or maybe absolution, but before Taylor could say anything they stopped again, and this time they were at the airport. "I'm sorry," Andi whispered, and then she was out of the car, taking her bags from the trunk. Taylor looked down and saw the folder with her art in it still there, and pushed open the door. "You almost forgot this," she said.

Andi looked at her, reaching out to take it, their fingers brushing in the process. "Thank you," she said. "I never would have forgiven myself."

"I would have found a way to get it to you," Taylor said.

Andi smiled. "I guess this is goodbye," she said.

"Have a safe trip," Taylor said.

"You too," Andi said. "I mean—"

"I know what you mean," Taylor said. She slid back into the car for the ride home, turning to watch Andi as she disappeared inside.

❧❧❧❧

It was the middle of the night when an alert popped up on Taylor's phone, telling her she had a private message. She slid her finger across the screen without thinking and was surprised when Andi's name popped up. It had been almost six weeks since the con, and although she sure as hell hadn't forgotten her, she'd done everything she could to put her out of her mind. Whatever Andi had been trying to tell her, whatever unspoken connection might have happened between them in the car on the way to the airport had passed. It wasn't ever going to happen again.

Taylor read the words on the screen once, then again, and then a third time convinced her eyes were playing tricks. "If I got you a ticket, would you come to see me?"

She typed her answer and clicked send before she could second-guess her decision. *Screw responsibility*, she thought. "Yes."

A flurry of messages went back and forth between

them. The next thing she knew, she was getting on a plane. She propped her head against the cabin wall as if she might somehow calm down enough to doze off and make up for last night's missed sleep. It was a lost cause, and she knew it, but she could pretend.

She was disappointed when she got into the car that had been sent to pick her up and found that Andi wasn't there. "She's on set," the driver told her as if he could read her mind. "Night shoot. She should be back at the hotel when you get there."

"Thanks," Taylor said. She hugged her bag to her chest as they rode, her fingers clenched in the fabric. At the hotel, she was given a key to her room, which was empty when she arrived. Andi wasn't there, and neither was any of her stuff. Of course, she wouldn't have invited Taylor to stay in her room. They barely knew each other.

She tried to settle in but ended up pacing until her phone chimed, indicating she'd gotten a message. "Just finished. Headed to the hotel now, but it takes a little while. Hope you had a safe flight. Can't wait to see you."

"Me too," Taylor sent back. Her stomach growled, and she realized she hadn't eaten anything since last night's dinner except for pretzels and those spice cookies you can only find on airplanes. She picked up the room service menu and discovered it was a lot fancier than she expected. Trying not to cringe at the prices, she called down her order.

She answered the knock at the door twenty minutes later and was surprised when it was Andi, not the food, standing outside. It looked like she'd tried to get the grime off her face, but it still clung to her hairline and around her nails. It made Taylor smile, and Andi smiled back. Then they were in each other's arms without Taylor knowing who had reached for whom.

"I can't believe you came," Andi whispered her breath ghosting over Taylor's neck, sending a shiver down her spine that settled in her core.

"I can't believe you invited me," Taylor replied. "You didn't say why." It wasn't exactly a question, though she was hoping for an answer.

Andi stepped away from her, but her fingers stayed hooked around the back of Taylor's arms. "It's just been a rough couple of days," she said. "Stuff happening on the show mostly…the plot, not behind the scenes drama. Dredging things up that I thought I'd forgotten, or gotten past, or…" She shrugged. "I didn't want to be alone anymore."

"I'm sure you have friends who—" Taylor was interrupted by a second knock at the door, and Andi turned to look, frowning slightly. "It's okay," Taylor reassured her. "I ordered breakfast." She opened the door, and they brought in two trays, setting them on the small table and leaving again. "I thought you might be hungry too."

"I am," Andi said, lifting the lid from her plate. "Oh, I love crepes."

"I know," Taylor said. "I mean, I read somewhere that you did. Do." Her forehead furrowed as she realized how that might sound. "Shit. Is that creepy?"

Andi looked at her, her eyes alight. "Maybe a little crepe-y."

Taylor looked at her sidelong. She was trying not to laugh. "Did you just…?"

"What are you going to do about it?" Andi challenged.

The spark that had been lit by Andi's embrace ignited. Taylor faced her full on, and she didn't hesitate. She closed the space between them, one hand coming up to Andi's face, the other sliding to her waist, and she kissed her. There was a fraction of a second where Andi was still, startled, and then her lips parted against Taylor's, and it was soft and slow and sweet and everything that Taylor had tried not to let herself imagine.

When they broke apart, neither of them released their hold on each other, so they were still belly-to-belly and hip-to-hip as they leaned back to look into each other's eyes.

"I do have friends," Andi said. "I wanted you."

"Past tense?"

"Want you," Andi amended.

"What are you going to do about it?" Taylor teased.

Andi's lips met hers again and long fingers tangled in Taylor's hair, and the entire world became only the two of them, just two girls and all the places their bodies touched, their ragged breaths mingling as they kissed.

"Breakfast is going to get cold," Andi pointed out when the need for oxygen finally became greater than the need to be as close to each other as possible.

"Let it," Taylor said, brushing her nose against Andi's before their lips met again. "I want you too. Present and future tense."

eternaleponine has been writing for as long as she can remember, and has been writing fanfiction for almost two decades. When she is not writing, she enjoys reading YA lit and training in Tae Kwon Do, where she has achieved the rank of second-degree black belt.

P.S. She's a Superhero

By Alexis N. Ramsey

Tara, it'll be fine. Mom loved Noie. She'll love Trish too!"

"Yeah, but Noelle's not a superhero!" Tara jolts when Trish touches her hip and presses a kiss to her hair. She hadn't heard Trish come in and she smiles over her shoulder and mouths "Ariel" while pointing to the phone.

"Excuse you, Noie is a hundred percent a su—"

"Sorry! Yes, yes, but that's not what I meant, and you know it! Noie's a superhero, a cop hero, but she's not an actual superhero! You remember what happened when I started using my powers!" She bites her lip. Bex hadn't exactly been thrilled by her new identity, and Tara isn't looking forward to explaining how she's now dating a superhero too. She opens her mouth to use her best whining phone voice on Ariel until Trish's hands trail up her sides to palm under her breasts.

"Oh, come on, she wasn't that bad, Tara. She even supports you with all her medical knowledge and lab now!"

Trish kisses the side of her neck, and it's hard to listen to what Ariel is saying. Her hands slip under Tara's shirt, and suddenly everything in the room is stifling. How Trish could rile her up so fast. Sol—

"Hey, Ariel, uhm, oh..." She feels Trish's smile

and grimaces as Ariel continues to speak. Trish always gets worked up after rescuing people, and her recent exploit, pulling a woman from a burning building that afternoon, had left her frisky.

"No, Tara, don't worry about it. Her and Trish will hit it off like old buddies. They both like…"

Trish bites at the soft spot below her ear and Tara nearly groans. She cuts Ariel off completely, and she'll probably get flack for that later, but right now she doesn't care. "You're probably right, Ariel! Bex will be fine, and it'll all go dandy."

She's spun in Trish's hold, and Trish presses flush against her. Noelle will make fun of her for days, but she hits the end call button for Ariel's benefit. Trish plucks the phone from her fingers and smirks.

"Mhh, that was taking much too long." She drops the phone to the floor and backs Tara toward their bedroom. Tara doesn't even look to see where her phone lands, she just backtracks and pulls Trish toward her.

Their first kiss is rough and fleeting, mostly because Tara trips and has to float to catch her balance. Their second kiss makes Tara moan. Trish tugs at her lower lip and urges her legs up, around her hips just in time for their tumble onto the bed.

And Trish isn't wasting time. She's still in her full costume, and the open-mouthed kisses she's trailing down Tara's neck aren't slowing her down. It's not that Tara finds sex while in costume hotter, but Trish's so amped up from rescuing that she's literally hotter. She's throwing off heat like a radiator to the point that even Tara can feel it.

She's never taken the human exaggeration of lighting the sheets up seriously, but she's almost worried at this point. Of course, as Trish works her shirt over her head, Tara realizes she only has a few options to avoid breaking the bed again.

"Up, T-Trish." She tugs at Trish's arm and shoulder, pulling her until she disengages from Tara's skin. She slides up Tara's body, confused until she catches sight of her eyes, then her eyebrows pop up, and she moves a whole lot faster.

She straddles Tara's head, wrapping her fingers around the headboard and Tara licks her lips. The black, spandex undershorts that Trish wears don't stand a chance against her fingers and Trish shivers at the sound of their popping seams. She's already dripping, and Tara hums before pulling her down and licking the arousal from her thighs.

"Oh god, yes." Trish is always vocal about her pleasure, and it's only gotten them into trouble a few times, most notably in a restaurant bathroom.

Tara hums again at the memory and trails her tongue through Trish's wetness, coating her lips. Her hips jerk down, and Tara tightens her hold on them. She sucks at Trish's clit, pulling a shudder and a moan from her. A fresh wave of arousal drenches her chin, and she follows it to Trish's entrance, working her jaw to press in as far as she can.

Trish cants her hips down, twitching against Tara's lips. "Ta—there! Tara!"

It's intoxicating, the rhythm Trish sets against her mouth, her taste, and smell, the feel of her, the sound of her blood pumping through her thighs, even the feel of her pants against her legs.

Not yet touched, she's soaked and hot, and her skin feels tight, and she wants Trish to come, shuddering and keening against her. She sucks harder, as Trish shouts. She pulls her tongue up to lave across the bumps of Trish's skin and Trish jerks in her hold.

There will be bruises on Trish's thighs. Tara's stronger when the sun is up, Sol. Tara just wants her closer. She juts her hips up, squeezes her legs together. Her clit throbs and she's distracted from Trish's arousal.

Consumed by the feeling of it, her blood pounds, resounding with the thrusts of Trish's hips. Each bump her tongue laves over, every cry Trish makes, all of their nerves joining where their skin meets drive her higher until she's desperate, desperate to have Trish coming apart around her.

She pulls Trish until Trish can't move her hips at all and sucks the arousal from her clit with a moan. Trish shudders until her muscles lock and she's crying out Tara's name. She jerks against Tara, twitching, nearly sobbing.

The blood rushes through her head and veins, driving Tara crazy. The taste of Trish on her tongue and the blinding heat of her body, something she can't feel from a human, push her fingers to her clit. Tara makes two circles before she speeds up her pace. She's slick, and her hips involuntarily jerk up.

Trish is still panting above her, dripping above her. She swipes her tongue through that arousal and Trish's cry drives her fingers faster. She's so close, and Trish is already grinding down again, shaking.

She blows ice across Trish's clit and sucks it into her mouth, humming as her fingers press into herself.

"Fuck-Tar-ahh." Trish clenches and shivers, jerking again as she peaks.

Tara doesn't take more than another second before she's curling around her fingers and groaning. She breathes out harshly, and Trish cries out again.

The sound of splintering wood barely filters into Tara's ears, and she doesn't pay attention to it at first.

She shivers and slowly blinks her eyes open. She hasn't let go of Trish's hip yet, so she pries her fingers open and gently rubs the area. She can't see the bruise from her vantage point, but there must be one.

Trish pulls away from her, and Tara looks up to see a flashing grin aimed her way. "Your lovemaking never ceases to amaze, my warrior." She pushes the splintered halves of the headboard apart, and, as they swing to the floor, Tara groans.

Every time Trish comes back from a mission! Trish may be rich from nearly a century of archaeological work and secret missions, but still! Headboards don't grow on...bushes? Vines? Human idioms...

Trish swings off her as Tara watches her breasts bounce. No headboard, but at least she has a nice view. Tara pulls her fingers out of her pants, and Trish glances down at the movement.

"Oh."

Her eyes flash, and Tara blushes. It's still early in their relationship, but this is Trish's fault! She came in all hot and bothered, and Tara couldn't help it!

Trish bends, so her lips brush against Tara's ear, her words sending goose bumps racing down her arms. "Oh, you are going nowhere tonight, Daughter of the Sun."

Her lips move south, sucking roughly against her skin and Tara gasps. What's a headboard every now and again? Trish's fingers slip between her legs as she takes Tara's left nipple between her teeth.

Tara's eyes roll back, and she groans, long and low. Heck, who needs intact beds anyway?

꙳ ꙳꙳ ꙳

"We leave today, yes?"

Trish's fingers trail through her hair, gently scraping nails along her scalp, drawing a hum of contentment from Tara. She doesn't want to think about how her adoptive mother will take the news that Trish also masquerades in spandex. Although Ariel is right, she warmed to the idea when she saw all the good Tara did.

"Yeah."

They stay entwined in their cotton sheets, on the side of the bed without the hole in the mattress, until Tara's stomach growls. She hears Trish's chuckle and groans. It's too early, even with the sun splayed across her legs, pouring energy into her veins. But Trish doesn't let her stay in bed. She does what none of Tara's other partners could ever do. Against Tara's will, she slings Tara over her shoulder and rises from the bed. The added pressure as Tara attempts to fly back to bed doesn't even put a fault in Trish's strides.

She tosses Tara into the shower, kissing her when she whines and heads into the kitchen. Trish's century spent among humankind has done wonders for her cooking skills. She starts with Turkish sausage. It's one of her favorites, introduced to her on an archeological dig. She buys it whenever she can find it.

It's sliced down the middle and searing in a pan in less than a minute. Next is brown rice spiced with lemon, ginger, and oregano. Its fragrance permeates the apartment as it boils. There are nearly six cups of it. She moves onto the eggs, deftly cracking half a dozen into a bowl and whisks. She adds flour and baking soda and more sugar than she cares for, but she's a sucker for Tara, so she makes the concession anyway.

The pancakes are dense. Trish chops Kalamata olives into them. They're close to the breakfast dish she remembers from her island home. Those were made with yeast and were cooked in a basket directly over a fire. She tried that, but the yeast available is wrong. This new version is sweet and savory and perfect for wrapping the sausage.

As the rice finishes cooking, Tara circles her waist with still damp arms and presses kisses to her neck. She always gets this reaction from Tara when she cooks for her. It's quite the incentive.

"You made my favorite," Tara whispers the words against her ear. Trish nods and presses back into her.

She knew Tara was nervous about meeting her foster mother with Trish in tow. There is nothing like good food to calm Tara down. Well, that and sweet, slow kisses, but that's a fix best left for days when they can lounge inside.

"When must we leave to arrive on time?" The rice is perfectly tender so, Trish grabs bowls and swats at the hotcake already held in Tara's fingers.

Trish was raised to become queen of her people and the fact that Tara couldn't follow the most basic of table manners was as irritating as it was endearing.

Any other day, she'd chase Tara and her hotcake down, and they would spend their day together, nude and sated. Not today, today she rolls her eyes and moves the hotcakes and sausages to the table. Tara can never stay away from the combo of flavors Trish presents.

"So? A time?" She takes seven sausages and twelve hotcakes and glares until Tara passes the rice. The pot's a little less than half full, but Tara can make that up to her later.

"Mh-maybeh uh-round noonish?" Tara fumbles out the words around a sausage.

Honestly, her mother would have an aneurysm over Tara's table manners. Trish shakes her head and throws a hotcake at Tara. "Mouth closed, darling. Are we flying or taking the car?" She flashes an innocent smile as Tara pouts at her.

Tara shoves the entire hotcake into her mouth, but, blessedly, chews silently. Trish waits. She's been alive for millennia. She can be patient. She takes a dainty spoonful of rice and winks at her tablemate.

"Hmph, if we fly, we can get lunch at the diner in Midtown." Tara grins. "They had the best milkshakes. I wanna see if they're still in business!" She takes her fifteenth hotcake and rolls another sausage in it before she looks up at Trish.

Trish shrugs, at least Bex will not have to feed them. Their appetites together can break a bank account. It would be rude to devour everything in Bex's house at their first meeting. "May their milkshakes be as they were in your memories." She raises her tea in a toast and Tara giggles before following suit.

❧ ❧ ❧ ❧

It doesn't take them long to pack and step off the roof of their building, Tara smiling into the sun, and turn toward Midtown. She hasn't been home since she started dating Trish and that feels like so long ago. It's been six of the most ridiculous and amazing months of her life, fighting together, loving together. It's like the sun permanently shines in their apartment.

She twitches and bumps into Trish, pushing her

into a barrel roll. The look Trish returns make her laugh into the wind. Anne City's seen very few villains since it gained the protection of yet another superhero and Tara's been free to pursue her freelance reporting and painting.

Bex has to like Trish. There's no way anyone wouldn't like her! So what if she can bench press a tank? That just makes her all the more perfect for Tara. They can't hurt each other accidentally. Sol, she can hug Trish as tightly as she wants to, and she can't injure the goddess. It's freeing like flying, casting off the control she craves.

The flight takes longer than usual. Their bags, wrapped in Tara's cape, can't take much over two hundred miles per hour. The landscape slowly transforms from desert to coastline, and they both dip low over the ocean to breathe in the salty air.

After an hour and a half, they slip into civilian clothes in a secluded stand of trees outside the diner. It looks the same as ever, and Tara nearly bites her lip in anticipation. She's going to get the vanilla, chocolate, and strawberry shakes. No, maybe the cookie one is better.

It's a difficult decision. Tara shares her concern with Trish as Trish pulls the door open. But a loud bang grabs their attention, and Tara whips her head up in alarm.

She watches as the bullet barely sails over her shoulder.

There are two men, one with a pistol and one with a sack held over the counter. Trish stops just out of view and Tara grits her teeth at the man with the gun.

"Get on the floor!" He waves the gun at her as

she stifles a growl. If she wasn't bulletproof…if, she was anyone else he could have killed them, and the fact sends rage racing through her veins, as she plans her next move.

But she's Star Sentinel in plain clothes, and she only kneels because Trish's already gone. She knows Trish will return soon. Heck, she'll probably land outside just in time to pluck the sack from their hands.

The man with the sack turns tail first, leaping right over Tara and into the parking lot. Just as Tara predicted, he doesn't get far. Eternal Savior takes his feet from under him, catching the sack of would-be stolen cash before it can even flutter open. He falls hard and groans where he lands, dazed. Trish looks up toward the diner just as a yelp sounds from inside.

She steps past Tara and freezes. The opportunity Tara's been waiting for arrives. Everyone's eyes are on Eternal Savior, so she slips backward and changes in a flash. Trish still hasn't moved.

"Get off me, you dick! I am not…" says a woman's voice.

"Shut up!" the man with the pistol shouts, jostling her in warning.

Tara frowns and squints through the diner wall. He has a hostage. A woman with his pistol aimed at her head. No wonder Trish had stopped. Even they would be hard-pressed to get to her before the bullet did, at least from this distance.

"You!" He brandishes the gun at Trish. "Back up, or I'll shoot! I'm leaving, and you're staying out of my way!"

Trish steps back, and Tara pushes off the ground, rocketing silently into the air above the diner. Trish keeps stepping backward. She glances at Tara and Tara nods. They can keep the woman safe together.

"Man, fuck you, I am not here to be some damsel…" says the woman angrily before the man cuts her off.

"I said shut up!" He pushes out the front door as Trish stops backing up. He stops after another step and fear flits across his face. "Back up! I'll do it!"

Tara's already descending when Trish steps forward. The man jerks back just in time for Trish's fist to close around the muzzle of the gun. Just in time for Tara's cape to flash in front of his face as she scoops the woman into her arms.

Trish crushes the gun, and the man screams. She punches him once, and he collapses. He won't wake up soon, but he will wake. The other man hasn't moved. He lays staring at them with wide eyes but makes no motion to rise.

Threats taken care of, Tara turns her attention to the woman in her arms. "Are you alright?"

The woman stares up at her, almost as wide-eyed as the man on the ground, and clenches her hands to her chest. He hadn't hurt her hands. Perhaps he'd bruised her shoulder? Tara looks at her skin closer. It doesn't seem to be damaged, but humans were so—

"I am in distress." Her voice comes out loud and Tara jerks a little. She can't see any signs of distress.

Trish walks over concern splayed across her face. "Here, allow me to see." She slips her fingers across the woman's cheeks and down to her shoulders. "You were so brave, to stand up to him. I applaud your tenacity."

"I'm in love with you!"

Trish freezes. Tara stares. Oh.

Ohhh.

The woman's face erupts into a blush, and she

shoves her hands over her face, practically punching herself. "Oh god. I'm so sorry."

She feels a rush of sympathy for the woman. Honestly, she's been starstruck before, and the woman had just lived through a near-death experience. Tara quirks a smile at Trish, but Trish isn't looking at her. She's watching the woman in Tara's arms with such fondness that Tara nearly blinks in surprise.

Trish reaches out to pry the woman's hands from her face. "Tell me, what is your name?"

Tara gently places the lady on her feet and rests her hands on her shoulders. She looks a little unsteady still. Trish has that effect on people. Even Tara still feels that same unsteadiness sometimes.

"Jess," Jess says, with her eyes toward the ground. Her blush hits her ears, and Tara grins.

"Jess," Trish states the name with a nod. "I can see the warrior within you. You are remarkable."

Jess raises her head, mouth open in shock, as Trish leans in to press a kiss to her cheek.

Tara sees the footage later, a surprisingly high-quality video of the gunman taking Jess hostage all the way until she and Trish wave at the diner owners and fly off with all six milkshake flavors. It covers quite a bit of the police officers' investigation as well. She's not at all surprised that the largest media corporation, the one she'd worked at for years, scooped the video.

The part provoking the most comments is what happens right after Trish presses her lips to Jess' cheek. Jess faints and falls back into Tara's arms. Tara's ears start to burn as she reads the comments that moment inspired.

❧❧❧❧

They don't make it to Bex's on time. They're an hour late. Tara saved half the vanilla milkshake as a peace offering, but she's not optimistic about it improving Bex's mood. She hates tardiness.

Bex's waiting for them on the back porch. She doesn't look particularly angry, and her heartbeat is only slightly elevated. That's got to be a good sign. They'd landed in a grove of trees, so maybe Bex hadn't seen Trish flying, not that it matters much. She knows Bex has a tracker on her, and Star Sentinel showing up with Eternal Savior at some podunk diner the same day she's supposed to arrive with Trish is far too coincidental.

"Tara, you really should call when you're going to be late." Bex meets them at the edge of the porch, running her hands over Tara's cheeks and shoulders. She straightens out wrinkles in the suit that aren't there and purses her lips.

The habit swirls warmth and affection through Tara's chest. It's been too long since she'd seen Bex. "Hi, mom." She wraps her arms around Bex and breathes out a sigh. She misses her first home on this planet, the familiar smells, and how Bex's heartbeat never fails to calm her.

Trish doesn't make a noise, just waits, standing behind Tara. There's a pang in her chest because she knows she and Trish will never get to see their biological mothers again, but she has Bex. Maybe, just maybe, Trish will get Bex too.

Trish may be over a thousand years old, but a family's still family, and she wants to share that with the woman she loves.

"So." Bex finally pulls back, but she keeps one

arm around Tara's waist. "Who is this woman I should have met months ago?" She prods at Tara's side, and Tara squirms even though she can't feel it.

Trish smiles and steps forward, extending her hand, introducing herself. "Patricia, or Trish. It is a pleasure to finally meet you Elizabeth."

"Oh gosh, no need to be so formal, Trish. It's Bex." She doesn't release Trish's hand. Instead, she steps forward to press her fingers on the inside of Trish's wrist. She hums and watches her watch.

Trish quirks her head at Tara, and it takes Tara half a second to comprehend. "Mom!" She goes vibrantly red and slaps her hands over her face. "Trish isn't some specimen for you to examine!"

"Oh, hush. I'm just taking her vitals. Forty, hmm, still in human ranges, but you run at almost the same temperature as Tara." She looks up at Trish and glances at Tara. "I assume since you were seen with Eternal Savior barely an hour ago, that you've somehow managed to woo an actual goddess."

Tara grows even redder, and Trish laughs. "It was I who wooed your daughter." She turns her wrist in Bex's grip and flexes, the muscles in her arm rippling to life. "Tara has told me of your scientific background. Would you like to measure my strength in comparison with your daughter's?"

Bex squints at Trish's bicep and nods. "Yes, and I'll trade you embarrassing stories about her." She waves at Tara and Trish with no attempt to hide her smile.

"Oh yes, I believe that will be most acceptable."

"What?" Tara gapes as Trish and Bex walk toward the house, arm-in-arm. "Hey! That's—Trish! Mom!"

Neither break stride, but their hushed laughter

makes Tara groan. This was a terrible idea. The warmth in her chest and smile at her lips won't save her pride, but maybe she doesn't need it if the people she loves can love each other too.

⁂

Bex's had Trish run on the treadmill, lift the couch, break a cinder block, and even give a small blood sample all while chatting lively about the shenanigans Tara got up to in her youth. Tara would mind a heck of a lot more if Trish stopped laughing, head back and full, or if Bex didn't promise her favorite meal for dinner, homemade pot stickers with a sweet sticky sauce.

Trish seems to take the poking and prodding well. Perhaps it's how effusive Bex is in her praise of Trish's prowess, or maybe she's just humoring Tara's mother. Either way, Tara falls a little harder when Trish's gentle or patient.

"Alright, there's a shower upstairs outside of Tara's old room, towels in the closet. I won't have you stinking up my furniture." She ushers Trish to the stairs and pats her back affectionately.

Trish hasn't sweated a drop, but she doesn't protest. The flight had done a number on her hair, and a warm shower would help her relax anyway. Besides, if Bex needs help with the ridiculous amount of pot stickers they're going to need, she should clean up.

Tara's lost most of the red in her face and quirks her head at Bex. It's not like her to banish a guest so abruptly. She just waves Tara to the couch. It's where they've had most of their hard conversations and Tara grimaces.

Bex waits for her to settle and then asks, "Does

she make you happy?"

Tara is taken aback for a second and doesn't answer. It's not the question she was expecting. But she nods, and Bex nods back.

"Do you make her happy?"

It's the day for unexpected questions apparently. Maybe this is what Ariel got with Noelle, perhaps that's why Ariel was so sure of Bex's response. "I think—I think I do."

Bex nods again and pushes out a rush of breath. "Well, good. I suppose that's all I can ask for." She stands and nods again, turning toward the kitchen.

Tara blinks and says, "You don't mind that she's also a superhero?" Could Ariel have called it so well?

She looks at Tara and sighs, "Yes I do mind."

Tara shrinks down. She knew it, knew she shouldn't have—

"But all of my other daughters are heroes too, so at least you can watch each other's backs." She rolls her eyes and Tara can't help the tremulous smile on her lips. "I don't know how I could have expected anything different after Ariel brought a cop home."

Bex moves to sit beside Tara, and Tara shuffles closer to Bex. "Thank you."

Bex presses a kiss to the top of her head and nods. "Besides, she can withstand your hugs and return them full force. She's perfect for you."

Tara smiles and nods, thinking of Trish's soft voice and their mornings spent snuggled together. "Yeah. Yeah, she is."

She listens to Bex's breath swirl in her lungs for a moment before pulling back. She couldn't have gotten more lucky, an alien on a strange planet, taken in by the best family. Her mouth gets halfway open to voice this when—

"Oh no." Bex raises her hand. "That's enough sappiness for one day. I have to head to the store. I'm guessing by her body temperature, Trish eats as much as you do."

A laugh bubbles out of her throat and Tara nods. "We once ate at a buffet till it was out of food for fun." She laughs even harder at the way Bex shudders.

Bex shoos her upstairs, so she's not in the way, but she knows it's to give her a moment to check in with Trish. Her bedroom hasn't changed much. A picture moved to her desk, a painting taken down... but largely the same.

Her fingers trail over a picture of Ariel, and she smiles. The door clicks shut behind her, and she turns to find a naked Trish wrapped in a towel. She grins and beams while Trish leans back against the door smiling.

"Alright, you two, I'm off to the store! Try not to tear the house down while I'm gone!" Bex calls from the stairs, and a second later Tara hears the click of the door.

"I assume this means I passed her tests?"

Tara glances back to Trish and rolls her eyes. "She was never testing you, well besides the actual tests to see what you can do physically. But, she just wants me to be happy." She smiles and steps forward, gently cupping Trish's face in her hands. "And you make me happy."

Trish meets her halfway for a sweet kiss and her stomach blossoms into butterflies. She feels as though she could fly, even without the sun.

"Well then," Trish whispers against her lips. "I believe this calls for a celebration."

Entirely different butterflies swirl much lower

than her stomach as Trish drops the towel. Trish's going to be her undoing, so quick to rile her up, and Tara can't bring herself to care, especially when her knees bump into the bed, and the incredible force behind Trish's strong hand pushes her onto her back.

Hot, wet skin slides over her body, as she thinks to herself, *who needs intact headboards anyway?*

Alexis is a twenty-two year old writer. She's written poetry for a decade and stories for fandoms for six years. She enjoys writing fluff and smut, detests angst, and would gladly die for soulmate aus. Currently, she participates in the Supergirl fandom. She loves to chat about writing and stories.

Season Finale

By Virginia Black

Jamie stood alone in the descending hotel elevator, giving her costume one last look in the door's reflection. Putting the outfit together cost half a month's pay, but it was money well spent. It matched the costume of her favorite television character perfectly, and fit Jamie as only custom tailoring could.

The character of Agent Denna Lopez wore a costume that was fully functional if the function was to demonstrate the wearer's fitness and physical proportion. Jamie had worked hard at recreating it and was proud of her efforts. A navy-blue vinyl top with a wide zipper down the front was cut to reveal the curves of her breasts. She tucked the navy-blue leather pants into her black leather boots. She adorned her waist with a replica of Lopez's electrified ceremonial blade, just like the one featured in a two-part episode halfway through the show's second season. A black shoulder holster held another replica weapon, and a fashionable, waist-length, blue leather jacket, cut to expose the handle of the holstered gun, completed the entire outfit.

Jamie tossed her long hair from her eyes, and it fell in strands over her shoulders and back in a straightened cascade that no cop, even one from the future, would wear on the job. Her hair wasn't the exact shade of bleached blond that Hollywood provided her character, but the summer months had given Jamie highlights pale enough to pass. She was grateful for the hotel's air conditioning. If she'd worn this outfit outside, she'd have collapsed in minutes in the Las Vegas heat.

The doors opened into the main convention expo floor, and the murmur of thousands of attendees welcomed her to her favorite flavor of geek madness, the fan convention.

Jamie strolled across the expo floor, head held high as she navigated the grid of over a hundred booths and tables. She was tall, with a swimmer's build like the actress on the show, and with her perfect match of a costume, devoted fans would recognize the character instantly.

A quick glance around the room took in various banners and giant cardboard cutouts of long-loved characters from all her favorite pastimes. The old-fashioned space opera shows she used to watch as a kid that had sparked her imagination, the comic books that helped her learn about herself all through her teen years, and the movies she binge-watched while stuck at home with a cold.

It was all here, all the imaginary worlds that helped her navigate her own life. She felt as much at home here, surrounded by strangers like her, as she did back in what everyone outside of this room called reality.

Though Jamie had attended dozens of fan conventions over the years, from those focused on genre science fiction and fantasy writers to big-name television and movie conventions, this one was her current favorite. "The Con For Us" was created by women for women and had a singular focus on popular culture featuring lesbian relationships in a healthy, positive light. And for the third year in a row, the stars of the television show *Improbability* were scheduled to appear.

Set seventeen years in the future, *Improbability* featured an ensemble cast of characters playing a fast-paced match of good guys against bad guys. The season finale had aired only two weeks ago, yet the show had already been renewed for another twenty-two episodes over the next year.

Improbability was a breakaway hit, highly rated for its political drama and psychological suspense as well as its sci-fi adventure, but most of the fans at this convention watched it because of its steamy romantic sub-plot. Agent Denna Lopez, a multi-national police agency's computer expert, had fallen in love with the enemy, international criminal and rumored assassin, Katja Mannis, known far and wide as the Falcon.

In just a few hours, both lead actresses, as well as the show's producers and showrunner, would be on the main event stage and would answer fan questions. Jamie saw the line for entry into the main hall stretched all the way across the main convention floor and out the expo doors into the corridor.

This year, the *Improbability* booth was the biggest one at the convention, crowded with fans buying T-shirts, autographed photos, buttons, and stickers. Jamie heard the excitement in their voices as they talked about the upcoming panel. Their enthusiasm was contagious, and she felt it as she drew closer to the booth. Several of the show's fans saw her outfit and approached her, asking her permission to take pictures. Jamie stayed in character as she posed for photos. Agent Lopez never smiled.

Logan had to be around here somewhere. She wouldn't miss this.

While Jamie dressed up as Agent Lopez, as she had for the previous two years at this con, Logan always dressed as her character's nemesis and the show's villain, Katja Mannis. Logan's costume was different every year, and Jamie wondered what would be new this time.

And then she saw her.

At the far end of the vendor lane, opposite from Jamie, a crowd of admirers surrounded Logan. Her costume was as implausible as Jamie's, but looking at it made Jamie's mouth water.

Logan's eyes met hers, and the game was afoot.

Clad from head to toe in matte black, Logan wasn't a perfect match for her character's runway-worthy looks. The only thing she had in common with her character was her long dark hair. What she lacked in matching features, she made up for in an ideally matching body type and drop-dead gorgeous features of her own.

Logan wore a skintight sleeveless top beneath a tighter leather vest that left her midriff exposed and showed way too much cleavage for daylight hours. Logan tucked body-hugging leather pants into square-toed boots with three-inch block heels complete with custom knife sheaths.

This year's costume had a new addition. The handles of projectile-firing weapons poked out the top of matching holsters tied with far too many straps to the outside of Logan's legs, below the curve of her hips, drawing Jamie's eyes to Logan's tautly muscled thighs.

Despite the amount of exposed skin, the character

never wore a coat. Jamie surmised that, evidently, villains didn't get cold in the future.

They stalked closer to one another, assuming the stance of their characters, while the other attendees cleared the space between them but crowded nearby. Today marked the third year they'd run into each other on the convention floor, and several people in the crowd knew what was coming.

"Katja Mannis," Jamie accused, in character voice, as she stopped a few paces away from Logan, though close enough to see the eager sparkle in Logan's dark brown eyes. "Not sure if it's daring or stupid for you to be out in the open like this."

Several of the con-goers cheered, as Jamie quoted the opening line from the last episode of the first season.

"Agent Lopez," Logan replied while wearing a small, sexy smile. "It's worth the risk just to see you in that uniform." She drew her eyes down Jamie's body and crooked an eyebrow.

Catcalls sounded from the gathered crowd.

"Let's cut the small talk," Jamie said and placed her hand on the handle of the plastic weapon in her shoulder holster. "And go for a ride to Central."

"Oh, I'd go anywhere with you," Logan said over more whistling and howling, her hands inching toward her holstered fake weapons. "But I'm not interested in lockup. Not for something I didn't do."

"I've seen the vids, Mannis," Jamie said. "You were standing over Renault's dead body. Don't waste your lies on me."

"Believe me. I wouldn't dream of it." Logan drew from both her holsters with fluid yet precise movement as Jamie pulled out her weapon, and they faced off, guns aimed at each other. The crowd cheered the end of the dialogue for a scene that, on television, had devolved into a long car chase.

Part of the crowd fell in around Jamie asking about her costume, and before she turned to answer, she saw Logan was once again swarmed with fans of her own.

By the time the crowd ebbed away, Jamie had looked around, searching for her pretend nemesis, but Logan was gone.

After a long day of walking the convention floor, taking photos with other attendees admiring her cosplay and with the actress who played Agent Lopez on the show, Jamie was ready to get out of costume.

At precisely 10:00 p.m., Jamie held her room badge up to the door scanner and waited for the telltale green light and accompanying click before opening the door. She slipped inside and let the door fall closed behind her.

"One move toward your comm, Lopez," Logan said in a low voice. "And I'll tase you unconscious. I guarantee you won't even feel the floor when you hit it."

Jamie froze, her heart pounding in her chest. She'd been waiting for this all day, and now that the time was here, she was so instantly aroused she could barely remember her lines.

Logan had spoken the first line from the last scene of the second season finale, a cliffhanger episode when the characters finally consummated the tension between them. The scene's dialogue was brief, but

Jamie didn't want to blow it.

"This is foolish, Mannis," Jamie said sternly. "The entire complex is full of agents. You won't escape this time."

Logan stalked closer, a replica of a futuristic weapon in hand. Her pacing matched her character's perfectly. "I don't care about the agents outside." She confiscated Jamie's fake communicator and replica service weapon and stashed them and her gun somewhere Jamie couldn't see. "Only the one in here."

Logan took another step closer to Jamie, and Jamie fought against her instincts, taking a step back as the character had done while moving closer to the wall. Logan followed her movement, closing the distance between them with each forward step.

"You know I didn't kill Renault," Logan whispered, inches from Jamie's lips. "You're smarter than the rest of them."

Jamie wanted Logan to kiss her, but it wasn't time yet. "I know what the evidence tells me." She sounded breathless and tried to calm down enough to get her lines out. "Renault's murder doesn't match the Falcon's M.O., and neither does the crime scene, but that doesn't mean you didn't do it."

"Yes, it does." Logan sounded angry, but her eyes said something else entirely. "And you know it."

Jamie heard a click and felt a new pressure on her wrists. She looked down to see Logan had secured her hands with a binding strap identical to the props they used on the show. To her surprise, there was little give in the binding. She was truly confined.

"Let me go, Mannis," Jamie said, as parts of her body tightened within the costume that now felt more restrictive than ever.

Logan moved her lips even closer. "I don't think you want that, Denna." She kissed Jamie hard and fast, then pulled back to look into her eyes for an answer to her unspoken question.

Jamie's heart raced as she looked at Logan with false indecision, then kissed her back just as hard.

This was where the show's original scene had faded to black, but Jamie was already wet, anticipating what she hoped came next.

Logan crushed her hips against Jamie's, pressing her into the wall and pinning her bound hands between them while easing the intensity of her kiss. Her tongue flicked at Jamie's lower lip, and then she bit Jamie gently as her hips pushed harder.

Jamie tried not to moan into the kiss. Logan moved her kisses to Jamie's neck finding every one of Jamie's exposed erogenous zones with her lips, tongue, and teeth. Quicker than Jamie thought possible, she felt ready for more. Jamie, fearing she'd forget the game, was suddenly distracted by the scent of Logan's skin mixed with the scent of her supple leather costume.

Logan pulled away and lifted Jamie's arms by the binding, pinning her wrists to the wall above Jamie's head. She kicked Jamie's legs apart and quickly unfastened Jamie's pants with her free hand. In seconds, she slid into the valley of the parted zipper, past the barrier of Jamie's boy shorts to the wet heat within, and then stopped, as if overcome by what she'd found.

Jamie was thrilled when Logan caught her breath and then skipped the pleasantries and got right to business, thrusting inside Jamie as much as the confining costume pants would allow. The sight of Logan focused on driving her senseless spiraled Jamie's arousal to new heights, as Logan moved from the skin she could reach to nip and bite through the costume at places still covered.

Jamie fought against the urge to speak, to encourage Logan deeper because there was no more dialogue to this scene. If she spoke, she'd break character, and the magic of this scene would end.

She didn't want that. She loved this game.

Jamie gasped for air as she felt the tightening of muscles that signaled impending release. Logan curled her fingers, and Jamie closed her eyes, slammed her head into the wall, and collapsed against Logan's waiting thigh, orgasm pounding through her body.

Before she could recover, before her legs could even hold her weight, Jamie felt the restraints around her wrists removed. Logan led her stumbling to the bed and raced to remove all of Jamie's clothes, then stripped off her costume.

Finally nude, they fell together near the center of the bed, Logan's hands pulling Jamie's hips to her own, their kisses urgent, Jamie's hands already searching.

❧❧❧❧

Jamie stirred when she felt a kiss on her cheek. The hotel room was still dark.

"See you next season," Logan whispered and nipped Jamie's earlobe.

The hotel room door clicked shut, and Jamie fell back to sleep.

❧❧❧❧

The next night, Jamie was back home after a long

day's travel across the country, her costume stashed in the back of her bedroom closet. Lying on her side in her bed, she faded in and out of consciousness until she felt the bed shift with the presence of another body.

"Hey, lover." Logan's voice sounded from the dark, and Jamie felt a kiss on her shoulder. "Sorry to wake you."

"What happened?" Jamie's voice slurred with exhaustion.

"I should have broken our rules and flown back with you. My second flight got delayed and then canceled, and I had to rebook in Houston." Logan pressed her nude body against Jamie's backside, her flesh cool but welcome. "I wanted to text you, but it was so late. I was afraid you were already asleep."

Jamie hummed at the soft feeling of Logan's skin against her own. They had traveled different routes and stayed in separate rooms at the con as part of the game, and she'd missed sleeping with her wife.

"Don't think you're getting out of taking the kids to school tomorrow," Jamie mumbled, wrapping Logan's arm around her tightly. She snuggled deeper into her pillow as she felt Logan's warm kiss on the back of her neck. "Agent Lopez has a date with the gym."

Virginia Black reads everything she can get her hands on, loves whiskey, and listens to electronica. She is writing her next angst-driven novel about two women who save the world by day but passionately love by night. Her first novella, BIG CITY BLUES, is available from most ebook retailers.

Going Down

By Rae D. Magdon

Leah didn't expect to see a demon when she stepped into the elevator. Sure, she'd noticed several cosplayers wandering the hotel during the past day and a half. They were here for *Girls Geek Out*, according to the signs in the lobby—or some weird television thing, as one of her more derisive colleagues from the New York branch had put it. Most of the attendees seemed to be excited college kids living off caffeine, their faces painted up and their waists cinched into uncomfortable corsets.

The demon, though. She wasn't a college kid.

She was tall for starters, tall enough that Leah had to tilt her head up to see her face. Beneath her makeup, the demon had dark, smooth skin, with translucent glitter to highlight the contours of her face. Elegant bat wings that looked like tissue paper, but seemed to be made of something stronger, extended from her shoulders and her exposed midriff was even more eye-catching thanks to the golden barbell in her navel.

Leah's gaze remained glued to the woman's midriff for an embarrassingly long time until the elevator dinged. She stepped forward, realizing she'd paused right in the middle of the doorway. Once she moved further inside, she squished herself against the wall, offering the demon and the other occupants a sheepish grin. To be honest, she hadn't even noticed there were other businesspeople and cosplayers until she had to squeeze past them.

Most of the passengers gave her sympathetic looks. Obviously, they didn't relish being in a crowded elevator that smelled like cologne and hairspray either. The demon didn't offer the same silent commiseration. She smirked, honest to god smirked, her heavily-outlined purple lips twitching up at the corners.

The subtle gesture made Leah's stomach flutter. *Don't look,* she told herself, training her gaze on a safer target, a balding businessman near the elevator buttons. *Don't stare. Don't make eye contact. Don't be a creep.* But her eyes refused to obey. They drifted traitorously to the left until Leah caught herself admiring the demon's long legs. Wrapped in sleek black stockings, Leah could see the shape of her legs through the sheer fabric.

By the time the elevator arrived on the first floor, a thin layer of sweat had sprouted beneath Leah's hairline. She wished she had chosen a lighter blouse, but she'd overestimated the hotel's air conditioning. That, or she'd underestimated how hot it would be in an enclosed space with a bunch of cosplayers, with one particular cosplayer.

The doors opened, and several people filed out, jostling to join the flow of traffic in the lobby. It was like a game of twister, and without meaning to, Leah found herself with a face full of wing and shoulder. The scent of lavender body wash filled her nose as she breathed deeper, pulling it into her lungs.

Oh. So that's how she smells.

Before she could reproach herself for the intimate thought, the demon was gone, heading for the front door. A long tail with a heart-shaped tip swished behind her, the same purple as her lips. Leah swallowed to work some moisture into her dry throat. She had a feeling she wouldn't be able to focus during her convention today.

⁂

The next morning, Leah waited for the elevator with a sense of wistfulness. She knew seeing the demon again was highly unlikely, but she couldn't help hoping. As she'd feared, the demon's mental image distracted her during most of her panels and workshops. She barely remembered anything from the sessions about alternative payment models and updated tax codes, but she could most definitely recall the playful glint in the demon's yellow eyes. Colored contacts, Leah assumed.

While lost in thought, the elevator arrived. The doors opened, and Leah's heart lodged in her throat. Her demon was back, only she wasn't a demon anymore—and yet, undeniably the same woman. This time, she dressed as an angel, with a short white tunic under gleaming golden armor. Miraculously, the armor managed to highlight the shape of her waist and her impossibly long legs without appearing ornamental. She had straightened her springy curls into loose ringlets, and she wore a delicate golden circlet on her head. There was a sword strapped to her back between her fluffy white wings, and for some reason, the weapon made her even more enticing.

Leah's mouth went dry as the woman stepped aside to make room. It was just the two of them this time, which wasn't fair. *Don't stare,* she told herself. *This woman is just trying to have fun at her con. A costume isn't an invitation to gawk.* And yet, try as she might, Leah couldn't look away. Her gaze locked with the beautiful stranger's, and Leah noticed that her eyes were a bright crystal blue.

"Which floor?"

Leah blinked. The angel's mouth was moving, but she couldn't make sense of the words.

"Or are you going to the lobby?"

Alarms blared inside Leah's head. Say something, say anything! "Um, lobby?"

"Sure." The angel withdrew her hand from where it was hovering in front of the buttons. Leah couldn't help but notice how slender and graceful it was, with long fingers that put plenty of wicked thoughts into her head. Thoughts about how those fingertips would feel against her skin, running down her belly, lower…

Their descent to the lobby could have lasted thirty seconds or thirty years. Leah wasn't sure, but she stared at the angel the whole way. By the time the elevator stopped, the nervous butterflies in her stomach felt more like a jet engine preparing for takeoff. Her pulse rate was revving without her permission.

The doors opened, and the angel stepped out, fluffy white wings bobbing behind her. Then, to Leah's shock, she turned and smirked. "Bye, Leah."

Before Leah could form any response, the woman disappeared, melting into the crowd until Leah could barely see the circlet bobbing away from her. For a moment, she was too stunned to exit the elevator. *Was she flirting with me? How did she know my name? Did she ask around or something?* Then Leah remembered the name tag hanging around her neck. *Oh. That was a dumb conclusion. The angel wouldn't circle the hotel asking questions about a perfect stranger. I'm the one thirsting here, not her.*

Still, the woman didn't have to address her at all, let alone use her name.

Leah pressed the open button as the elevator began to close, bustling out before she ended up taking a ride back upstairs. She was going to have an even less productive conference than yesterday, she could already tell.

⁂

Leah smoothed her dress, wishing she'd thought to try it on before packing it in her suitcase. Hanging in her closet, it had looked like a great choice for the Sunday night appreciation dinner. Now that she was wearing it, she noted the fifteen pounds she'd gained over the past couple of years. Doing up the zipper had taken some acrobatics.

My clothes just don't want to work with me, Leah thought. *Not like the gorgeous cosplayer. I bet she could pull off a paper bag.*

But it certainly wasn't jealousy she felt when she remembered the woman's outfits from the previous two days. The demon and the angel cosplays had both looked stunning, and Leah kept wavering on which was her favorite. She'd spent an embarrassing amount of time going over the details in her head instead of taking notes.

Leah secretly hoped she'd be able to see the woman at least one more time. If she were lucky, maybe they'd head for the lobby at the same time Monday morning. It was unlikely, but—

"Going down?"

The sound of a low voice made Leah start.

She whipped her head around, eyes widening as she realized who it was. "You?"

The demon-angel was standing right behind her, although she wasn't dressed in either of those cosplays anymore. She was wearing something in between, ragged black wings, feathered as the angel's had been, but colored like the demon wings. She wore silver armor—Leah was very appreciative that it showed her stomach—and carried a whip coiled at her hip. Her face was painted with purple shadows under her eyes, as though someone dragged their oily fingers down her cheeks, or as if she'd cried through the world's thickest mascara application. Her hair was back to its natural springy state but sprayed white, and her eyes were bright red.

Leah's draw dropped. It was a beautiful costume, worn by an even more beautiful woman.

"Uh…"

The woman gave her a crimson-lipped smile. "I guess I can be 'you' or 'uh,' but why don't you call me Azrael?"

Leah tried to form words, but her traitorous tongue had already twisted itself into a nervous knot. "I, uh—I don't know where your costume is…from?"

Azrael arched an elegantly shaped eyebrow, which had been painted the same white color as her hair. *The Third Heaven?*

"Never seen it. Is it good?" *Christ, what a lame thing to say,* Leah thought as soon as the words slipped out. *Could you be any more awkward?*

"Played it." Azrael seemed amused rather than disdainful, which only made the churning in Leah's stomach worse. "It's a video game."

"Ah." Try as she might, Leah couldn't think of

a response. She stood there for a stupidly long time before realizing she hadn't even pushed the button. "Sorry," she mumbled once the light came on. "You showed up and I, um, forgot."

"We all get convention-brain by the end of the weekend. What are you here for?"

"D.B.C. Diversified Business and…" Leah's voice trailed off. She wasn't a flirt, but this was pathetic even for her. "A bunch of boring business shit my boss is making me go to."

Azrael's red eyes sparkled. "That bad, huh?"

Leah sighed. "Sixty-two of the seventy speakers were white men over forty. I counted."

"Lucky them, I guess."

The elevator arrived, dinging as the doors opened. Azrael stepped inside while Leah's brow furrowed. "Wait, what?"

Azrael stopped between the sliding doors and smirked. "Because they'll get to see you in that dress at your party?" She stepped the rest of the way into the elevator, and the doors began to close.

Leah took a breath. This was her chance, stand here like an idiot, or seize the moment. She chose to seize the moment. She rushed into the elevator, joining Azrael inside. As the doors shut, Leah realized just how close they were standing to each other. There were only six inches of space between them. Leah tilted her chin up, barely able to breathe. Azrael was looking down at her, and she found herself lost in those burning red eyes.

"Leah?"

Leah forgot to breathe. *Oh god, she remembered my name.*

"I hope I'm not reading this wrong, but can I kiss

you?"

The question punched the air from Leah's lungs. Had Azrael just said that? Shit. She really just said that. Azrael was still gazing at her, waiting patiently for an answer.

When the elevator lurched into moving, Leah moved too. The signals firing from her brain finally reached her frozen muscles, and she angled her head, presenting her lips. Azrael's head dipped, and Leah stood on tiptoe, hoping her knees wouldn't buckle.

Azrael's mouth was hot. Hot and sweet. Her lips tasted like lipstick, but Leah didn't mind. The fact that she was kissing a beautiful stranger more than made up for it. Despite her wandering thoughts for the past several days, she'd never imagined this would happen. But it was happening. Azrael's tongue swiped gently along her lower lip, and Leah opened to grant her entrance.

Her tongue didn't taste like lipstick, and soon Leah was sucking on it eagerly. She ran her hands up along Azrael's arms, which felt thin but strong beneath her palms. Azrael's fingertips grazed the small of her back, pulling her closer, and Leah gasped into the kiss. They burned through the fabric of her dress, leaving the skin beneath warm and tingly.

The ding of the elevator shattered the moment. They broke apart, and Leah pulled back. The doors opened, and she could see several people in costumes and formal attire milling about in the lobby. Azrael didn't move. She leaned against the wall as if waiting for something. Leah's feet remained rooted to the floor. She couldn't find the will to step away from Azrael, let alone leave the elevator and head to the party.

After several long seconds, the doors closed

again, and the elevator started rising. Leah didn't consciously remember reaching for the button to her floor, but it didn't matter. Azrael was kissing her again, and the warmth of their joined mouths seeped through her whole body to pool straight between her legs. When she scrabbled to press number twelve, her hand slipped. It fumbled over the stop button, and the elevator shuddered to a halt.

Azrael pulled back a few inches, looking down at her in surprise.

When Leah realized what she'd done, she grinned sheepishly. "Screw it. There are two others people can use."

Azrael laughed. "I like the way you think."

Their mouths crashed together again, hot and hungry. Leah grasped Azrael's shoulders, accidentally tilting her wings off center, and Azrael's hands ran down Leah's sides, gripping her hips and pressing her more firmly into the wall. A whimper slipped from Leah's mouth as she felt Azrael's knee slide between her legs. It was a little awkward thanks to her tight dress, but the pressure still felt distractingly good.

Holy shit, I'm really doing this, she realized as she rocked forward into Azrael's thigh. Things were going at light speed, but she couldn't help it. Opportunities like this rarely came along, and Azrael was offering her the perfect surface to rub. Her clit sparked each time she moved her hips, soaking her panties in a matter of seconds.

Azrael didn't seem to mind. In fact, she encouraged the movement by hitching one of Leah's legs around her waist. That caused Leah's dress to ride up, but she was well past being embarrassed. She'd already tripped on her tongue several times, and by some miracle, this gorgeous woman was still interested in her. She wasn't about to question it.

Soon, Leah was grinding shamelessly above Azrael's knee. With nothing but her panties between them, she was sure Azrael could feel her wetness. She tried to focus on the kiss, to pour herself into that instead and slow things down just a little, but her hands had other ideas. They ran along every inch of Azrael's body she could reach, finding gaps in the armor and searching somewhat unsuccessfully for flesh.

She didn't make much headway with the shortened breastplate, but the bare skin of Azrael's stomach did give her a little room to play. Leah shuddered as hard muscle flexed under her fingertips. Azrael was tall and slender but full of hidden strength. Leah suspected she was an athlete or at least a regular at the gym.

With a low growl and a gentle nip to Leah's lower lip, Azrael pulled back. Leah chased her mouth, disappointed, but her noise of protest turned into a groan of pleasure as Azrael bent down, cupping her rear in both hands and hefting her off the ground. She threw her arms around Azrael's neck, holding on tight.

Azrael's abdomen was even better to grind than her thigh. Leah whined through a string of kisses, bucking forward as much as Azrael's weight would allow. Pinned, the sensation of helplessness only turned her on more. When she looked into Azrael's eyes, there was softness behind the colored contacts. She seemed happy, but when she noticed Leah staring, her brow furrowed.

"This is okay, right?"

Leah almost laughed. It was more than okay, but she appreciated the inquiry. She answered with another kiss, getting in a nip of her own and raking her nails down Azrael's back. That sent Azrael's wings further askew, but Leah managed to find a short patch of flesh to scratch beneath Azrael's neck. Azrael shuddered so hard that Leah could feel it too, and she noted that move as a success.

She would have explored further, but the ache in her core was becoming a distraction. Her muscles clenched, and Leah realized with some surprise that she was close. She'd never come just from grinding against someone. *Then again, I've never had sex with someone in an elevator either.* The thought should have scared her—and it did, a little—but the moment consumed her. They'd already come this far, and Leah didn't want to stop. Just the thought sent an almost painful pang through her lower belly.

Azrael seemed to sense it. "What do you need?" she asked, breaking away from Leah's lips to whisper in her ear.

Leah moaned as Azrael nipped the lobe with blunt teeth. She couldn't get any words out at first, but eventually, she managed one. "Fingers?"

Azrael shifted her hold, using her weight to pin Leah more firmly to the wall so she wouldn't have to use both of her hands. Leah did her best to help by hanging on, but she forgot all about it when Azrael's hand cupped between her legs. Suddenly, those gorgeous fingers she'd been admiring were dipping under the waistband of her panties, sliding down to test her wetness.

And there was a lot of wetness. Azrael inhaled sharply, kissing a grin into Leah's mouth. Leah could tell she was pleased, and that caused her inner walls to flutter as she coated Azrael's fingers with another surge of slick heat. Azrael took full advantage. Her fingers slid up and down at first, seeking sensitive spots, but soon zeroed in where Leah needed them most, right on her clit. The swift circles Azrael made left her dizzy, and she buried her face in Azrael's shoulder, breathing in the scent of lavender.

Oh fuck. She feels so good. Too fucking good.

"Please," she whimpered aloud, although she wasn't sure what she was begging for anymore. Just more.

Luckily, Azrael knew better than she did. With a few more strokes to Leah's clit, she abandoned the swollen bud and dipped down to Leah's entrance. Leah waited for Azrael to push inside, but it didn't happen. She seemed to be waiting for something—permission, Leah realized dimly. She gave it by rolling her pelvis, taking Azrael's fingers inside herself. They slid inside without any resistance, and Leah hissed as they hooked into her sensitive front wall.

"How hard do you want it?" Azrael asked, her voice throaty with want.

Leah pulled away from the crook of Azrael's neck and stared straight into her eyes. "Hard."

Azrael appeared more than happy to oblige. She started moving her fingers, thrusting shallowly, curling more than pumping. The friction was intense, and Leah's eyes blurred. The colors around her smeared together, but she could still make out Azrael's white hair, dark skin, and purple-painted face. She covered it with kisses, not caring where her lips ended up, ignoring the taste of body paint. She was too far gone to process such minor details.

The fingers inside her were magic. They seemed to know exactly where Leah needed them, and Azrael's thumb came to rest on her clit before she could even ask. She yelped as it pressed against her, massaging roughly through her hood, but she hooked her legs tighter around Azrael's waist. No matter how intense this was, she didn't want it to end.

"Gonna," she panted, attempting to offer a warning. "Gonna...come..."

"Come," Azrael murmured, half ordering, half pleading.

That was what did it. More than the fingers stroking her and the thumb rolling over her clit, Leah was overwhelmed by Azrael's unique mixture of confident dominance and gentle consideration. Spots of white flashed at the edges of her eyes, and she cried out, clenching around Azrael's knuckles.

The ripples of her release hit harshly, crashing over her with the force of a tidal wave. Her whole being trembled, and something within her burst as she spilled over into Azrael's hand. It was a lot of fluid, more than Leah was expecting, but Azrael took it in stride. She kept going, and Leah threw her head back against the wall, sobbing her relief to the elevator's ceiling.

Her mind kept jumping around like a needle caught on a record. *Oh god full harder faster more yes keep going.* She didn't realize she was saying any of it out loud until Azrael swallowed the words with one last kiss, muffling her cries and fucking every last bit of tension out of her.

Leah's peak tapered off far too soon. She slammed back into herself, still squeezing sporadically. The ache inside her was gone, soothed by the pleasant stretch of Azrael's fingers, but her limbs were still tingling with electricity, and her thundering heart showed no signs of slowing down. "Wow," she said, breaking into a breathless laugh.

Azrael laughed too. "Yeah. So, my room?"

Leah didn't even have to think twice. "Definitely." Then she remembered she'd hit the elevator stop button. It had seemed like a clumsy but smart mistake at first, but now, it presented several problems. "If we can actually get off."

"I'm pretty sure you got off." Carefully, Azrael withdrew her fingers and lowered Leah back to the floor, steadying her while she regained her balance. "My name's Alexis, by the way."

"Alexis," Leah repeated, testing the name out. "Sexy."

"Not as sexy as Azrael, but I'll take it." Alexis glanced at the buttons with a slight frown. "So, is there an elevator go button, or...?"

Leah was disappointed to find there wasn't. Her only option seemed to be a speaker system labeled *press here to talk*. She pushed, and the speaker crackled with faint white noise.

"Hello, this is security."

Only then did Leah realize she had no idea what to say. She was also acutely aware that the elevator smelled like sex, and anyone who came to restart it would almost certainly notice. *No way around it, though. We can't stay in here all night.* Leah blushed as her mind raced with possibilities. If they were stuck in here all night, she doubted she and Alexis would have trouble occupying themselves.

"Hello? Is anyone there?"

"Sorry," Leah blurted out. "We hit the stop elevator button by mistake. Can we get someone to restart it?"

Alexis snickered, and there was a sigh from the speaker. *"Don't worry, ma'am,"* the employee on the other end said in a flat voice. *"Happens all the time. I keep telling management to update things and get rid of the button. Someone will arrive in about ten minutes."*

"Thanks," Leah said. A click came from the speaker, and there was no more noise.

"Ten minutes," Alexis drawled. "What are we going to do until then?"

Leah turned and grinned, pressing Alexis's back into the wall. "I can think of a few things."

Alexis's white painted eyebrows rose in delighted surprise. "You think you can make me come in ten minutes?"

Leah licked her lips, dropping to her knees and sliding her hands up Alexis's long legs. "I don't think," she said, with confidence she hadn't felt before. "I know I can."

Rae D. Magdon is an author of queer, lesbian fiction. Her stories celebrate lesbian, bisexual, queer, and trans women falling in love, and she cares deeply about representing communities of color. In addition to publishing novels about all kinds of women and their adventures, she has an extensive fanfiction collection available online.

A Wavelength in Indigo

By Kayla McCall

Riley arrived at DimenCon early on Friday morning. She'd been saving her paychecks from Walton's Big and Tall for months to purchase a plane ticket to New York City. Even though she wasn't big or tall or a man for that matter, the store paid above minimum wage and let her work long hours when she wasn't going to class. The target audience for the store were customers who typically didn't know or care that much about fashion so Riley could keep most interactions short and have a happy customer out of the store with a whole new wardrobe in under thirty minutes.

Today, the retail chain was out of Riley's mind as she walked through the entrance of the venue hosting DimenCon 2018. Riley was already dressed in her Indigo cosplay, having changed into it right after getting off her flight and she barely had time to breathe as she dropped her bags off in her room before she was booking it two blocks east to the convention.

She didn't know where to go, and she stepped around the many patrons on the city sidewalk as politely as she could while simultaneously staring down at the directions on her phone. She'd never been this far away from home on her own or at all for that matter. She went to college locally. The farthest north her family had been from Alabama was Tennessee, and she had to beg her mother not to force her older brother to go along with her as the most misguided chaperone from the entire south.

But she was here now, and she had to hold in her excitement as she passed by other people dressed in matching dark green leather jackets, sleek black pants, and bright yellow trainers. The ugliest combination out of context, but anyone who knows *Dual Stream* would recognize all of them as the main character, Indigo Zaveri.

Collin, Riley's brother, who read the trilogy purely out of spite after hearing her gush over it was the one who suggested she cosplay as that specific character just because he thought that Riley and Indigo shared the same level of bitchiness. Riley didn't believe Indigo was a bitch, maybe just a little misunderstood. Never mind that that's usually the tagline for the antagonist.

"You are the best Indigo I've seen so far, albeit I haven't seen that many just yet." That came from a tall guy that looked like he could have benefitted from a shopping trip at Walton's. Dressed as Fritz, Indigo's best friend, his cosplay was on point down to the curly red wig on top of his head.

"An evil ginger?" That was a line often spoken from Indigo to her best friend, and it made the man in front of her smirk. Riley was secretly pleased by his compliment. She knew that Indigo and herself had more than just their bitchiness in common. Indigo's skin color was a dark, dark brown. So much so that there was a purplish-blue undertone to her skin color which was probably how the author, Bette Morrison, came up with her name even if she promised that there was more to it than that. Anyway, Riley shared a very similar skin color and overall physical stature so although she played around with the idea of cosplaying as another character, her fate was sealed way before she purchased her ticket to the convention.

"What's your name?" Riley asked him.

"I'm Jeremy." He stuck out a hand, and Riley shook it before giving him her name. "So, which book is your favorite out of the trilogy?"

"Oh, definitely *Ornamental Elements* when Indigo meets herself from the second dimension, but my favorite part was when she met Carter from the second dimension." Riley laid her hand over her heart and bent her head back. "I ship it so hard." Carter is the main enemy throughout the trilogy, trying to capture and study Indigo to exploit the ways she can travel through dimensions, but within the second dimension, Indigo completely falls for Carter and Riley completely fell for that relationship.

"Indigo was so smitten for her in that damn book." Jeremy rolled his eyes. "She was like a completely different person. The second dimension Fritz was just a complete idiot though."

"Morrison wrote an entire chapter from his perspective where all he did was ponder if stepping on a hoe would make it swing up and hit him in the face."

"I do like how she ended that chapter though! We just read him stepping on it, and then the chapter closes and then in the next one Indigo finds him with a concussion."

"Fritz is such a gem," Riley smiled.

"I am representing primary dimension Fritz here today at this convention. Here, in New York City."

"So you say, but you sound a lot like the second dimension right now."

He laughed. "I like you. And since you're such a

Cartigo slut, I think I know the perfect Carter to your Indigo."

He didn't give her a chance to respond before grabbing her arm and pulling her along behind him, deeper into the convention. There were hundreds of people around, most people in cosplay, but a fair amount weren't wearing costumes. The whole place was decked out in *Dual Stream* themed decorations. They even had two areas of the venue marked off as primary and second dimension respectively. The decorations in the primary dimension were all indigo, even the lightbulbs had a blue tint and the second dimension was decorated in red.

Jeremy came to a complete stop somewhere in the middle of the red room, standing on his toes to help him see over the crowds of people, but he was already so tall that the effort seemed unnecessary. Once he found what he was looking for, he started walking again, but the farther they got, the thicker the crowd became, and there were several times that Jeremy almost lost his grip on Riley's arm.

When they did come to a stop, it was in front of a girl in Carter cosplay, a very military type look with camo pants and a white V-neck T-shirt, with a toy knife strapped to the side of her leg. She had sandy-blonde hair, light brown skin, and green eyes that were staring at Riley with a kind of childish excitement. Before she was able to process what was happening, the girl grabbed her face and planted a kiss on her lips. It wasn't a quick one either. Her lips were pressed against Riley's for a good thirty seconds before she pulled away. If this girl wasn't so beautiful and Riley wasn't so gay, Riley would have pulled away a long time ago.

Riley was so caught up in the moment that she

forgot to be confused after the girl pulled away. She didn't say anything she just stared at the girl's muddy green eyes. They were like a swampy green, but they were beautiful to Riley all the same.

"Indigo, hello!" She said, and then Riley remembered that this interaction mirrored a scene from *Ornamental Elements* when Indigo first met Carter from the second dimension. Carter came up to kiss her, but Indigo was sure she was going to attack her, so she had a knife hidden behind her back and was ready to stab her if she had to, but when the girl kissed her, the knife clattered to the floor.

Once Riley regained control of her voice, she coughed out a greeting to her.

"*Lo siento.*" She rolled her eyes at herself. "Sorry, sorry." She had a thick Spanish accent.

"It's okay," Riley replied, still actively trying to keep her shit together.

"*Me encanta esa escena del libro.*" Riley stared at her for a moment, realizing that the reason she couldn't understand her, was because she was legitimately speaking Spanish.

"She said she loves that scene from the book. This isn't the first time she's done this today." Jeremy shrugged, and Riley's smile dropped just a little. "I thought you could use a proper welcome to DimenCon, so I brought you to my favorite Carter."

Jeremy was standing between Riley and the girl. She was smirking at Riley with a kind of mischievousness that she couldn't place.

Nonetheless, she stuck out a hand towards her. "Hi, I'm Riley."

"Alessandra." She said taking Riley's hand in her soft one. "I get a little...excited at conventions."

"I can tell. I don't tend to complain when a pretty girl kisses me."

"*¿Qué dijo ella?*" She directed the comment to Jeremy, and he translated. When he was finished speaking, Alessandra blushed.

"She doesn't speak much English, but she knows more than she lets on," Jeremy said. "I did make sure she knew the word convention before we came here."

"How long have you guys known each other?" Riley asked.

"A few years ago—"

Alessandra cut him off. "We met on the the… internet. *Me hizo venir a la convención.*"

"I made her come to the convention. I coerced her from her little house in Spain from thousands of miles away. I even bought her plane ticket."

"*Tengo suerte, él no es un asesino loco.*"

"She says she's lucky I'm not crazy," he laughed.

"I don't know, if you're second dimension Fritz you might be a little crazy." That made Alessandra laugh, and she rubbed her hand down Riley's arm.

"Were you planning on going to Morrison's panel?" Jeremy asked Riley.

"Of course. She's my favorite author."

"Great. You can sit with us. We should go now if we want good seats."

Alessandra smiled and locked her arm around Riley's, and they all started walking with Jeremy on her other side. She looked up at Jeremy and whispered, "*Me gusta esta chica.*"

⁂

Morrison's panel was amazing, but all Riley could focus on was Alessandra. She was very forward in her advances. Riley knew enough Spanish to translate what she'd said to Jeremy. Throughout the entire panel, Alessandra was holding Riley's hand and brushing her fingers over her knuckles. This wasn't anything that Riley had ever experienced before. She'd only had a few tentative romances with maybe a girl and a half since she'd been in college if that was even possible. Before that, her only girlfriend had been in high school. She dated Amanda for almost two years, and they broke up right before graduation because she decided to go to college in New York. Riley thought about that a lot during her flight to the convention no matter how much she tried to shift her attention elsewhere.

Before they broke up, they were inseparable. Riley gave her credit for being her first love. They were best friends first, but after Riley came out to her in a McDonald's parking lot, Amanda surprised her with a confession of her own, and before Riley could even process what was happening, they were making out in Amanda's car. She'd nearly had Riley's shirt off before they were shooed away by an annoyed pimple ridden employee. Their relationship was the definition of u-hauling without being able to u-haul at all. Still, they'd sleepover each other's houses and stick around each other at school. Amanda was there when Riley came out to her mom and told her they were dating. The downside, their sleepovers were no longer allowed. When their senior year ended, and Amanda left for college, Riley lost her girlfriend and her best friend.

Alessandra was interesting, and Riley was intrigued. Even the one and a half girls she dated in college didn't come on to her that quickly.

After the panel, Alessandra kept ahold of her hand and pulled her behind her and Jeremy. They were in the indigo room when Riley decided to talk to her.

"I know you're from Spain, but where exactly?"

"Um, I am from Cudillero, Asturias. Small and color…colorful. I love it. Maybe I'll take you there someday." Riley didn't notice the goofy smile that started to spread across her lips. "¿De *donde eres?*"

"I'm from east Alabama." Riley shrugged. "Nothing special."

"Oh! *Me gusta tu acento.* I thought it was different than the normal American accent that Jeremy has." She brushed her thumb over Riley's knuckles again as she talked.

Riley swallowed the lump in her throat and said, "So, which book is your favorite?"

Alessandra paused a minute, probably translating the words in her head the best she could. "*Uh, me gusta el primero libro.*" She shook her head and laughed a little to herself. "The first book is my favorite."

"Cool."

"Yes, um…" She reached up and tugged on Jeremy's wig from where he stood a few paces away to get his attention. "*Dile que me gusta Carter en ese libro. Me gusta lo malvada que es.*"

"She adores Carter because she's evil, much like herself."

"So, she's into primary dimension Carter?"

"Oh yeah, for sure. That's her costume."

"I thought you were second dimension, Carter?" Riley asked her incredulously.

Jeremy translated and then listened to her response before telling it to her. "She wanted you to think that, but Carter is Carter, and she loves both versions of her. Don't worry. She ships Cartigo as much as the next guy."

It isn't a huge deal, but Cartigo meant a lot to Riley. She read *Dual Stream* before she came out, before she started questioning. The idea of being gay was something she pushed to the back of her mind. Random people at her high school would ask her if she was a lesbian and even though she had no idea, she'd always say no.

It wasn't until she came across this book series in her school's library while skipping lunch that she sat down and allowed herself to consider the possibility. That was when she was in ninth grade and by the time she was a sophomore, she was finally able to say it out loud to herself, and by the beginning of her junior year, she was telling her best friend.

"Hey, can I take a picture with you guys? You're the best Cartigo pair I've seen." That came from a girl who looked to be a few years younger than Riley. She was probably still in high school.

"*Sí, sí.*" Alessandra said, beckoning the girl over. She handed her phone to Jeremy and went and stood to the right of Alessandra and Riley was on the left. Jeremy counted down from three and right before he got to one, Alessandra turned her head and kissed Riley on her cheek.

❧❧❧❧

By the end of day one of DimenCon, Riley was sure that Alessandra was emitting hormones that were making her high because she somehow thought it was a good idea to go back with Alessandra to her hotel room. Jeremy was there too, but none of her focus was on him. There was a blackout party that night hosted by the convention and Alessandra convinced her to go back with them to change. Since Riley went to New York on her own, she didn't plan to go to the party, and she didn't pack any black clothes besides the pants she was wearing for her cosplay. Alessandra was letting her borrow some of her clothes.

Their hotel was in the opposite direction of the convention venue and Riley's hotel. Maybe it was the pace they were walking? Or the fact that Riley was more focused on Alessandra than her own feet moving over the pavement? She suddenly noticed Alessandra was still holding her hand and leaning her body into her own. Every few steps their arms would brush, and their feet would bump into each other midstride.

When they finally arrived at the hotel, Riley learned that Jeremy and Alessandra had separate rooms. Which made complete sense considering the convention was the first time that they were meeting in person.

"I'll meet you guys in the lobby in about twenty minutes?" Jeremy said, and both of them nodded and went to Alessandra's room. It was at least fifteen minutes later, and Alessandra still had Riley pinned up against the door, kissing her. Riley was sure Jeremy would be waiting quite a while.

Alessandra slid her hands up and down Riley's torso. She was getting worked up and had to pull her mouth away several times to catch her breath.

"*Sabía que te gustaba desde el principio.*" Alessandra breathed in between kisses. "I liked you… from the beginning."

Something was nagging at the back of Riley's mind. "Jeremy said you kissed other girls dressed as Indigo?"

Alessandra pulled away and sighed. "I did. With a few girls and I am sorry, but once I saw you, I…sent Jeremy to speak to you."

Riley's mouth dropped. "You planned all this?"

"I saw something I liked." Before Riley had a

chance to respond, Alessandra was kissing her again. Riley gripped her hips and pushed off the door and eased their bodies over to the bed their lips still joined in a kiss. She had Alessandra under her for a full two minutes before someone was banging on the door.

A few ragged breaths later and Riley was able to push herself off of Alessandra and over to the door.

It was Jeremy, of course. And his red wig was removed to reveal a dark fringe. "When did twenty minutes turn into thirty?"

"¡Lo *siento, Jeremy!*" Alessandra yelled from her spot on the bed.

He stuck his head inside the room and surveyed both of them for a second. "Were you two getting it on? Cartigo style?"

"I prefer Alley, *gracias*."

"Alley! Okay, I'm down, I ship it. You two have fun!" He waggled his eyebrows before pulling the door closed behind him.

Through all that, Alessandra hadn't moved from the bed. When Riley turned back towards her, she stretched her hands out and said, "Come back."

Riley walked back over and reclaimed her spot on top of Alessandra and planted a firm kiss on her lips. "*Me gusta esa chica.*"

"*Me alegro.*" Alessandra whispered back as she pulled her lips back down to meet her own.

Kayla McCall has been writing and publishing stories since she was nine years old. She has placed in the Scholastic Art and Writing Awards as well as the PTA Reflections contest. She recently published her first novel, Finding Lights, and she is currently studying English-Creative Writing at Auburn University.

Risen Phoenix

By Akemy "Curly" Ortiz

The first time Sarah saw her was like something out of an 80's rock video. Her imagination was making the gorgeous woman move toward her in slow motion to a song from some hair band. She approaches, seductively smiling while unbuttoning her suit jacket just as a fan turns on, striking a sultry windblown pose.

The olive-skinned beauty looked ravishing in a runway-ready business suit, tailor-made to her body, in a pinstriped jacket with her credentials hanging from its breast pocket. Even her dark brown hair was cut exactly like the character's debut season, reaching just below her ears.

She didn't dress like the characters featured at this new small convention. In fact, one might think she was a rep for the hosting hotel, or maybe an agent for one of the talents. Sarah knew who she was supposed to be. She was looking at an extremely subtle representation of DA Kimberly Risen. Half of her favorite dynamic duo and doppelganger to the RNIS star in work mode, glasses and all.

Sarah looked proudly down at her own clothing choice for her character's counterpart, Phoenix Zamora, the confidential informant and all around streetwise badass. She was subtle in her season two choices today as well, ripped, faded blue jeans, a flannel wrapped around her hips, and a white tank top, proudly showing off her muscular arms.

To complete her dedication to playing the character, she had forgone the wig this year and bleached her hair. Shaving the right side of her head in small striped patterns, just like Phoenix. She adorned her right bicep with the exact tattoo of a little black cat with bright yellow eyes that the actress had in real life, and was written into the show.

Before spotting tall, dark and gorgeous, Sarah had not seen another reference to her fandom. Their pairing wouldn't be headlining at this con. Her OTP was only a ship in her mind and the subtext obsessed minds of their other fans. Every smile and touch between the characters sent fan message boards into a frenzy of memes and fiction writings.

She tried to stay close to her fandom mate, hoping someone spotted her with the same amount of enthusiasm she was feeling. However, when they did end up running into each other, it was quite literal and more than once. Sarah, convinced she had pissed off a higher power, watched as that beautifully annoyed smile became equal parts condescending and sincerely threatening.

It started when Sarah trampled over her coming out of the ladies room. Helping her up and trying to apologize, she was stopped with an angry, dismissive sneer. As fate would have it, they ended up attending a lot of the same panels, too. In one, Sarah had managed to snag the last seat in the front row, forcing the seething woman three rows back. Sarah felt eyes burning into the back of her head for the rest of that panel.

Later in the day, Sarah thought maybe the

capricious beauty had left early since she hadn't spotted her for some time. Then she stopped to take a drink from a water fountain, only to discover it broken as it shot her newly acquired hot nemesis square in the face with a stream of water. The wad of paper napkins Sarah quickly grabbed from the bar was snapped out of her hands with an angry huff before she watched her storm off. Again.

༄ ༄ ༄ ༄

On the second day, Sarah caught her last name, Martinez. Martinez was disagreeing with a bartender, and loudly challenging the terrified girl's competence until a manager showed up to talk her down from filing a formal complaint.

It would have all been appalling and intimidating, save for the fact that the formidable woman dressed like a nun that day. Making the entire scene quite entertaining to bystanders, who only saw a nun, with the mouth of a sailor, yelling at a bartender.

Sarah, dressed as a stereotypical nerd with high-waders, pocket protector, and glasses, unintentionally dressing to match Martinez again.

What's in this Punch, was season three's Halloween episode. This episode was cherished by all Risen Phoenix fans, as their favorite should-be-canon couple shared a long hard kiss. It was all for the con they were playing on a fraternity drug smuggling ring, but it sent their fan base through the roof.

In the show, the duo played into the kiss to draw the attention of a group of drunken frat boys away from a detective sneaking into their house. The heated looks before and after the intense kiss had gone viral by the next day.

Sarah's little gay heart had hoped for this con experience, where she would meet a girl who was as into her favorite show as she was. But her instant crush on the mysterious Ms. Martinez diminished, as it had proven impossible to stay on her good side the first day. Sarah decided avoidance was the best option.

Later in the day, that task proved impossible as more attendees recognized their cosplay costumes. They found themselves pulled into numerous photos together. More than a handful of people believed them to be a real-life couple, spurring a look of fierce annoyance on Martinez's face.

After a couple of hours, they both seemed to accept the fact they could not avoid each other. The attention from their fandom had a calm and uplifting effect on both of them, and they began to have fun. They played into their characters for fun poses. A nun and a nerd with their hands wrapped comically round each other's throats or wearing dark sunglasses, trying to look hard-core. They even posed as if a couple of girls dressed in black tactical gear, were arresting them, which caught the eye of the official Con photographer.

To Sarah's dismay, she lost track of Martinez early in the afternoon. She had searched the main hall for her but left to attend the last writing panel of the day. Her eyes were straying continuously toward the door in hopes of seeing her enter.

When the panel ended, Sarah quickly ran to her room to change, so that she could enjoy the hotel's pool in the early afternoon sun. She sunbathed until the sun began to set, then jumped into the water for a quick refresh before heading out.

Coming out of the pool, she retrieved a towel

and leaned over to begin patting her hair dry. With the towel still over her head, her elbow struck something hard, and she heard a loud yelp followed by a splash. Pulling the towel off her head, she saw a woman at the bottom of the shallow end of the pool. There was a red tint beginning to spread in the water. Without hesitation, Sarah jumped in.

By the time the lifeguard reached them, Sarah was making her way over to the side with the woman carefully balanced in her arms. Having spent a few summers as a lifeguard herself, Sarah knew to keep her as level as possible, making sure to support her neck until a board was brought over. To her relief, the unconscious woman began breathing on her own, but the small gash on her head was bleeding badly.

Twenty heart-stopping minutes passed until Sarah saw beautiful brown eyes open and look at her, nearly gasping when she recognized her cosplay adversary from the con. Sans makeup and in a striking black bikini, she was now sporting a neck brace and a bandaged head while a paramedic took her vitals.

Sarah knew she couldn't follow in the ambulance. After all, she didn't even know Martinez's first name. So when they moved to take her, Sarah simply squeezed her hand. Her heart jumped when she felt a small tug back.

⁂

The next morning, Sarah woke hours before the convention began, wired and anticipating the biggest day of events. Convention Saturdays always included headliners, competitions, and prizes. Too early to get dressed, she headed down to the diner for an early breakfast.

"Can I get you some more coffee?" The waitress asked Sarah while she sat at the bar.

"One to go, please. And the bill."

"Your bill's covered, hon." The older woman handed her a travel cup of coffee and motioned behind her.

Sarah turned to see a woman seated at a booth, a cup of coffee nursed between her hands and an uneaten muffin in front of her. Ms. Martinez, a small butterfly bandage on her forehead, sat gesturing to the seat across from her with a smile in invitation.

Taking her coffee, Sarah thanked the waitress and approached the booth cautiously. "You're…"

"Nina Martinez." She said quietly, offering her hand. "And you're my nemesis from the convention and the pool."

Sarah laughed nervously and shook her hand. Trying to be smooth, she said, "You mean the pool I helped pull you out of."

"More like the pool you knocked me into." Nina teased with a short laugh. "What I mean is thank you for jumping in after me, Miss?"

Fidgeting with the strings of her sweater, she stammered, "Sarah. My name's Sarah Kidd."

Nina motioned again to the seat across from her. "Well, Ms. Kidd. The EMTs last night told me what you did. When I saw you here, I figured at the very least I owed you breakfast after saving me."

Sarah took a seat, placing her hands anxiously around her to-go cup on the table. "Please, call me Sarah."

"Okay, Sarah."

The way Nina said her name made Sarah's body

shiver involuntarily.

"And it was nothing. As you said, I was the one that knocked you in." Sarah's kind face showed concern. "You're okay, though?"

Nina nodded. "I'm fine. The doctors were initially worried I might have had a concussion. So they monitored me for a bit, but they cleared me relatively quickly. Just a little cut that bled like a shark attack apparently."

"It sure did." Sarah guffawed. "Scared the hell out of me."

They took each other in silently. Sarah watched Nina push a strand of hair behind her ear. A habit she noticed the first day at the con, but seeing it this close sent her a bit off kilter. With only a subtle touch of blush and lipstick, wearing jeans and a green flannel, Nina looked comfortable and adorable.

"I'm glad I caught you here this morning. Obviously, I planned to look for you at the con, but this way," Nina flipped her hair dramatically, "we can speak in private without all our fans constantly interrupting."

Sarah chuckled at Nina's impression of a snobbish tone. With a flourish of her hand, she played along. "At least the paparazzi are leaving us alone. We simply must fire our bodyguards dear, and get new ones. Bigger ones."

"Agreed, darling." Nina sat up straighter, placing a hand daintily to her neck, making them both laugh.

Sarah tapped her coffee cup with Nina's. "We could totally have our own show. Awards all around."

"I'd thank you in my speech." Nina laughed at Sarah pretending to fan herself like she was going to cry. "Oh, stop."

She quit her antics, feeling her chest tighten and her head go light at making Nina laugh again. The flirtations and smiles they shared gave her hope that their initial clash was far behind them.

"You know, I thought I met everyone that dressed like Risen Phoenix at these cons, but I know I've never seen you before. You've truly looked the part these last couple of days. I mean, you could be her stunt double."

"Thank you. I could say the same about you, especially with the hair, and that tattoo!" Nina motioned to Sarah's arm. "Now that's commitment."

"Thanks," Sarah said, playing with the tips of her hair.

Nina bit her lip for a moment before confessing, "I admit I'm a bit of a late bloomer to the show. It was my resemblance that made me start watching, but I fell in love with it."

Sarah's eyes had focused on lips that were nibbled on nervously before speaking. Completely enthralled by their shape and movement, she hadn't realized she was staring until those lips began to stifle a laugh.

Sarah quickly took a drink from her coffee, shooting her eyes across the room. "So, is this your first time dressing the part?"

She missed Nina's appraising eyes as she answered, "Actually it is. This is also my first convention. I flew in from LA by myself."

Sarah finally looked back, hearing a city very close to her home. "Big city girl."

She winked at Nina, quickly admonishing herself at the stupidity of her actions, and blushing all over again.

"I'm in Long Beach myself," she tried to recover. "But I'm originally from Boston."

"I've been there. It's beautiful, especially in the fall." Nina took a small bite of her muffin. "So, I take it this isn't your first time dressing up as my CI?"

"No. Not at all." Sarah pulled out her phone to show Nina her collection of pictures from different cons.

She watched Nina flip through the photos, laughing at a few of the more comical poses, and wowed by the number of celebrities. Sarah shrugged off the admiration, inwardly thrilled she had impressed her.

"I've dressed like other characters from different shows, but I've been doing Phoenix since RNIS started. Of course, I used more wigs back then because I had short hair."

"I must say I like the natural approach you have now. Much more realistic and true to form." Nina returned her phone and then reached across the small table to run her fingers through a lock of Sarah's hair hanging down her shoulder.

Sarah forgot to breathe. Feeling the heat of a hard blush move up her face to highlight the stupid grin she couldn't stop.

"I can say the same," Sarah stammered, relieved and elated to see hints of pink appear on Nina's cheeks as well.

"Thank you."

Sarah relaxed. "I'm happy we're the only ones dressed like them here, though. Every other convention with the RNIS gang, you would have had a ton more competition of cosplayers dressed like Risen. Men and Women."

Nina coughed out, "Seriously?"

"Yeah." Sarah laughed, "Imagine our run-ins times a couple of hundred Kim Risen and Phoenix

Zamoras."

"No thank you." Nina snickered. "I believe one of you is quite enough."

Sarah attempted a deep breath to keep herself from doing or saying something stupid but instead triggered a coughing fit when she saw Nina give her a flirtatious once over.

"Are you alright? Do you want me to get you water?" Nina offered before smiling wickedly, "I can squirt it in your face if it would make you feel better."

Sarah's cough turned into a laugh, enjoying the new ease of Nina's company.

She straightened in her seat, "Listen, Nina, I feel I should apologize for you getting hurt yesterday. I am glad you're okay."

Nina stopped Sarah with a gentle hand on her arm. Both of them jumped from a tiny shock they felt at the contact, but Nina did not remove her hand.

"I'm fine, and I'm the one that needs to apologize for my behavior when we first met." Nina released a happy sigh, "Plus, I must confess I ended up having a lot of fun yesterday."

"Me too." Sarah grinned. "And I swear I didn't know that water fountain broke."

"I know you didn't," Nina released her arm to swat Sarah's hand playfully. "I can't believe how many pictures we took together? Do you know how many phone numbers and propositions I received yesterday?"

Sarah smirked, "I got twenty-six."

"Forty-seven," Nina exclaimed.

"Holy crap!"

"Ten while I was in the habit!" Nina made a face bugging her eyes out.

"Seriously?"

"I know!" Nina covered her face with her hands, trying to hide her blushing. "I don't think I could claim that in the span of my life, let alone a couple of hours. I have no idea how."

"Are you kidding me? Have you seen you?" Sarah said before thinking, her eyes going wide.

Nina dropped her hands back to the table. Now grinning, she replied, "On the contrary. I've been too busy looking at you."

Sarah could only surmise that her expression turned into that of a young girl who was talking to her crush for the first time because that's exactly how she felt. Willing her body to regulate itself enough to attempt to play things cool, she knew she was in desperate need of a timeout. Deciding to take the easy way out, she looked at her watch.

"I hate to say this, Nina, but I'm going to the *Detroit Chronicles* panel first thing today, and I still have to get dressed."

Nina jumped to her feet. "Oh my goodness, I didn't notice the time either. I have to do the same." Nina stood and placed a tip on the table, watching Sarah out of the corner of her eye. "You know, I'm attending that panel too."

"Oh?" Sarah said trying to cover her eagerness to continue Nina's company after a reprieve. "Did you get early seating?"

"I did," Nina said in nonchalance, leading their way out of the diner.

"Maybe we can meet at the hall entrance and make a line for the panel together?" Sarah paused, stuffing her hands nervously in her tight jeans but making eye contact.

Nina reached for a strand of Sarah's long hair

again, twirling it between her fingers. "See you there at eight?"

"On the dot." Sarah nodded absentmindedly intoxicated by the beautiful woman playing with her hair.

After Nina walked away, Sarah whimpered, "She's killing me."

❧ ❧ ❧ ❧

She made her way down to the entrance of the con, wanting to get there before Nina to not make her wait. Luckily her outfit today didn't take long to put together.

She was dressed like Phoenix Zamora in the sixth season promotional posters, wearing a red tank top, black skin tight jeans tucked into heavy boots, and a red bandana wrapped around her right thigh. All topped off with Sarah's prized possession, a replica leather collarless motorcycle jacket. Her blonde hair was brushed over to the right, and her eyes lined with dark shadowed makeup.

When she and Nina spotted each other, they couldn't help the laughter that escaped from across the foyer. Nina was in the dress from the same season's promos. It was a deep aqua blue colored dress that hung off her shoulders and gave a generous view of her cleavage, finished off with deadly looking heels that added a couple of inches to Nina's height.

"You do pull it off very well."

Sarah felt a surge of confidence as Nina appraised her body. She took a step closer to whisper hotly in her ear, "Play your cards right and you can pull it off too."

The seductive tone of her voice had the desired

effect on Nina, as she watched her cheeks pink. What she didn't expect was for Nina to pull her back in by the lapels of her jacket and whisper back.

"That…" Nina took two steps back with a smirk on her face. "Was super cheesy."

Sarah shrugged her shoulders before following her with a goofy smile. "I try."

They attended two of the same panels together that morning and got to know each other more, chatting between the sessions and waiting in line. They discovered they lived only about an hour from each other in LA time. They both had a fondness for movie screenings in the parks and a preference for visiting the beaches at night.

While they were buying buttons at a stand, whispers began circulating that a famous, recently out actress had shown up as an attendee. They made their way to the panel she was spotted attending. Nina smooth-talked her way through the closed panel doors so they could sit two rows behind her to covertly take a picture. Both of them froze like deer in headlights when the actress made eye contact with them and smiled.

After lunch at a small café down the street from the hotel, they decided to walk to a nearby park that included a small duck pond. Sarah watched Nina's eyes shine with childlike glee when she had spotted two swans.

"I've always loved swans, such beautiful grace. I wish I had thought to get bread at the cafe." She pouted.

Sarah produced two slices of bread in a napkin. "Bam."

"Where did you get that?" Nina asked excitedly.

"I bribed the waiter after you suggested coming here." Sarah shrugged, handing Nina a slice.

"You are just full of surprises." Nina gave her a sincere smile.

They took turns throwing pieces of bread into the water, feeding the inhabitants of the pond until it was all gone, then moved to sit on a nearby bench.

Sarah noticed Nina shiver, and without skipping a beat, she shrugged off her jacket to wrap it around her shoulders.

"Thank you," Nina said as she pulled the jacket that was a few sizes too big for her, tighter around her body.

Sarah grinned. "You're swimming in it, but it'll keep you warm."

"Oh? I don't know." Nina stood and pulled the jacket completely on, zipping it close. "I think I look pretty badass, don't you?"

Sarah laughed harder at the woman whose dress was now almost covered by her favorite jacket.

"Oh, sweetheart. I don't know what's more adorable, you saying badass or trying to look badass in heels." Sarah motioned to Nina's feet.

"You don't think heels are badass?" Nina placed her hands on her hips sauntering back to Sarah. Leaning slowly down to whisper in her ear, "Try walking around a con all day in them."

Both of them laughed as Nina moved to sit back down on the bench.

"Soooo." Nina drew the word out as she shuffled a bit closer, once again taking a strand of Sarah's soft blonde hair, and keeping her eyes focused on it. "You think I'm adorable?"

Sarah flashed her crooked dimpled smile. "Yes. An adorable badass."

Nina's laugh came out in a snort, and she bit her

lip through an embarrassed smile. Sarah laughed with her and scooted closer to cup her cheek.

"Also very beautiful." She added, stroking the soft skin with her thumb.

They moved forward together, meeting for a gentle kiss, letting their lips linger pressed against each other. Sarah placed two more soft kisses on her lips before leaning back, catching Nina licking her top lip with a laugh.

"What?" Sarah's brows furrowed.

"Are you wearing bubblegum lip gloss?" Nina licked her lips again, laughing more.

Sarah pouted. "I like bubblegum."

"Now who's being adorable?" Nina reached for Sarah's chin and squeezed it, leaning back in for another brief kiss, deepening it this time.

Sarah hummed, "Would it be too soon for me to ask if you'd like to go out with me sometime? Maybe once we're back home? I don't live that far."

"A date does usually come before the kissing, but..." Nina stared at Sarah's lips. "I would like that very much."

Sarah's eyes moved to Nina's temple and saw the small bandage hidden by her hair. Leaning forward, she placed a tender kiss on the spot.

"Stop fretting. I know it wasn't on purpose." Nina cupped Sarah's face this time, bringing her eyes back to her own. She squinted skeptically. "Or was it?"

Sarah huffed, "Oh totally. It was all part of my evil plan to knock you unconscious and trick you into a date."

"I thought so." Nina kissed her again.

"So no permanent damage, then?" Sarah asked, her face still held gently in Nina's hands.

158

"Well, that is yet to be seen. We haven't even been on a date yet." Nina gave her a contemplative look. "I do believe you could destroy me."

Sarah's eyes sparkled with a mischievous grin. "I think I could say the same."

They leaned into another kiss, letting it deepen naturally and wrapping their arms around each other. It was Sarah's turn to shiver. Not from the chill of the afternoon turning into evening, but the chills Nina induced from her body.

❧❧❧❧

Three Years Later…

"Nina, where the hell is my leather jacket?" Sarah yelled while frantically searching inside the hall closet.

"What leather jacket, dear?" She heard Nina call out from their bedroom.

"Nina Martinez, you know damn well which jacket." Sarah closed the closet door and made her way down the hall. "My favorite jacket that you haven't let me wear since they canceled RNIS. The one I was wearing the weekend we first met."

When she reached their bedroom doorway, she froze. On their comfortable grey duvet was her gorgeous girlfriend wearing nothing but the missing leather jacket, unzipped and hanging seductively off of Nina's shoulders as she lay enticingly on her side.

"This one?"

Sarah's dimples pierced her cheeks. "Yes, that one."

She kneeled on the bed, Nina moving to mirror her position across from her.

"I thought we were going to dinner."

Nina wrapped her arms around her girlfriend's shoulders. "I canceled."

Sarah ran her hands down Nina's naked sides. "Now why'd you go do that?"

The jacket fell off Nina's shoulders and hung on her arms. She leaned forward and in a deep timbre voice whispered, "Because when I thought about how I wanted to celebrate our anniversary, being in public was the furthest thing from my mind."

Sarah's body shivered at her words and the feather-light touch of a nail trailing up her arm. She wrapped her arms around Nina's waist and pulled her into a deep kiss, sliding her hands to Nina's bare ass and squeezing to bring their hips closer.

"Still want your jacket?" Nina asked with arched brows when they pulled apart for air.

"Nope." Sarah pushed her back on the bed, kneeling between Nina's legs, and taking in the gorgeous tanned skin that was all hers.

"Thought so."

"I love when you wear my stuff." Sarah leaned over Nina, supporting her body with hands on either side. "I'm having a flashback to my 80's rocker chick fantasies of you."

"Ever the charmer, my love," Nina said as she pulled Sarah down on top of her, kissing her hotly. "Now, show me what you did to those groupies in your fantasies."

Sarah grinned and moved to Nina's side, leaving a leg draped over hers, and running soft circles on her girlfriend's stomach. "I will do exactly that, if and when you do a striptease to a song of my choosing."

"What do I get in return?" Nina teased, moving her leg over Sarah's jean covered hip.

"You want something shiny, don't you?" Sarah teased Nina's thigh.

Nina's glee when she received jewelry was one of Sarah's favorite things in the world. Her girlfriend loved jewelry of all kinds. It didn't have to be 24k gold or diamonds, as long as it had made Sarah think of her, and it sent Nina off to find the perfect matching outfit.

A pair of long intertwined looped earrings for her birthday were matched with an off the shoulder dress for a nice dinner. An anklet for Christmas paired with red capri pants and a sleeveless polo shirt for an evening walk on the pier in the summer.

And a simple gold cuff bracelet for their first anniversary that secretly read "To My Adorable Badass" on the inside? Well, that night they went no further than Nina's kitchen counter.

"I think I need a necklace this time. Maybe something with a sapphire." Nina said as she pulled Sarah's shirt off, then bra.

"Deal." Sarah began kissing Nina's sternum, groaning when she unbuckled her belt and unzipped her jeans.

Sarah felt nails scratched lightly down her back before hands were tucked in the back of her jeans to cup her ass. With their conversation and dinner forgotten, they made love.

Hours later, Sarah lay with her head hanging off the foot of the bed, giggling as Nina tickled her feet. She moved onto her elbow to look at her girlfriend sitting up against the headboard.

"If you react like that every time, I do believe I have a newfound adoration for this jacket." Nina laughed as Sarah moved to join her by the headboard. "Why were you looking so intently for it anyway?"

Sarah kissed her nose, "Because I hid your gift inside the chest pocket."

Nina squealed with excitement, immediately reaching into the pocket to feel around for her present. She froze.

"Sarah?"

Sarah moved Nina's hand and reached inside to retrieve the ring. Sliding to the floor, she turned Nina to sit at the edge of the bed and kneeled between her legs.

"Nina, these last three years with you have been pretty damn amazing. I never thought I'd meet someone like you, let alone at a con. We've survived them canceling the show that brought us together. We survived dating long distance when I had to go back to Boston last summer. I didn't kill you after moving in together, and you didn't run for the hills after meeting my parents. I love you like crazy, baby. And I want to be with you until we're too old to make love the way we just did without dislocating something." They laughed together. "Marry me, Nina?"

Nina was only silent for a moment before she tackled Sarah to their bedroom floor, laying kisses all over her face.

"Is that a yes?" Sarah asked.

"Yes!"

Curly is a fiction writer from Southern California, where she lives with her High School sweetheart and Wife of 18 years, Rachel. She, along with her close friends Terri and Debbie, encouraged this endeavor. Curly believes in peace and love through art.

Lost and Found

By L.K. Early

Full disclosure, I'd had my eye on the Professor long before that night. For instance, I knew that she had the apartment directly over my tattoo parlor and that she'd complained once to the landlord about me playing music past midnight. I'd heard other things from the other tenants that she taught something science-y at San Francisco State and that she was from Paris, France. And of course, there were the things I'd seen for myself, that she liked to buy flowers across the street, that she liked to wear black, and that she liked to smoke cigarettes out on the sidewalk while she waited for her ride to arrive. She went out often and came home late. Sometimes with a companion, sometimes alone, sometimes with a man, and sometimes a woman. So yeah, I guess you could say I was intrigued.

That night it had been a slow night, and I was just about to close up shop. The air was heavy with an expected rain, and I'd hoped I could get home before the storm. I was locking up the safe in the back room when I heard the little chime on the front door.

"Bad news!" I called. "We're closed."

I listened, expecting to hear the door open and close again. But I heard nothing. I grabbed my bag, turned off the office lights, and poked my head out. That's when I saw her, standing by the window, staring up at the tattoo designs on the wall. She smiled to herself, her head cocked to the side, her fingers resting gently on her mouth. I watched for longer than was polite, but I couldn't help myself. I'd never seen her this up close before. Her blond curls settled down over her shoulders as she leaned back to look at the wall. I cleared my throat.

"Sorry. Hi. Can I help you?"

She turned, surprised by my voice. She smiled. "Oh, I'm so sorry. I just...I have a favor to ask. I'm Justine. I live up there." She pointed at the ceiling. "Over you."

"Hi. I'm Christina. I work here." I reached out a hand. "Under you."

She blushed and shook my hand. "Pleased to meet you."

"The pleasure's mine." I held her hand a little longer than was necessary. She was older than I thought, with lovely smile lines at the corners of her mouth.

She blinked and looked away like she was nervous. "Ehm, I lost my bag tonight, which, as you can imagine, had my entire life inside it."

"Shit. Bummer."

"Yes, and that includes my keys and my phone and my money, and I know this is awkward, but could I use your phone? Or could you call Leighman, the landlord, for me? I don't know how else to get inside my place." Her lip trembled, but I couldn't tell if it was from the cold or something else.

"Of course!" I pulled out my phone. "But it's kind of late. I mean, he might not—okay, it's ringing." I listened as it rang and rang. There was no answer. "I'll text him."

"Oh, thank you so much."

She walked back to the window at the front of the store. She gazed out onto the street as I texted. After texting the landlord, I joined her.

"Merde," she said. "It looks like it's going to rain."

"Listen, you can wait here for a little bit. I'm not in a hurry. Maybe he'll call back."

"He's probably asleep in his bed, which is where I should be. I don't know why I keep going to these stupid intellectual parties. Just a bunch of stuck up snobs anyway. I'm too old for all the posturing." She paused, standing up straighter, puffing her chest out. "You know what I mean?"

"Sure."

"No matter how intelligent men are, it always comes down to a pissing contest, doesn't it?" she said.

"Maybe you're going to the wrong parties."

She let out a little laugh that was closer to a sigh. "Maybe."

"Speaking of which, I have a better idea. Instead of waiting here, let's head down the street to Wild Side to get a drink. Have you ever been?"

"Wild Side? I don't think I know it."

"Perfect. Let's go."

"Oh, I couldn't. I don't have any money."

"It's on me. Besides, if we stick around here too long, we're going to have to deal with drunk dudes looking to get a tattoo to impress their girlfriends. If you think you're sick of posturing now, just wait until one of those guys shows up."

She glanced out the window again. The sky was a typical shade of San Francisco gray. "Those clouds above us certainly look ominous."

"Oh, I don't know." I pulled open the front door. "I'd say they were more autumnal than ominous."

She smiled. "Autumnal...I like that word. But I'm curious, what's the difference?"

"A thunderstorm in summer is ominous, but a thunderstorm in autumn is romantic."

"Well, I guess I can't disagree." She tucked her hands happily into her coat pockets and joined me at the door. "And I guess one drink won't hurt."

The bar was pretty crowded for a weeknight, but we managed to find an empty table along the wall. I was tempted to offer to take her coat but stopped myself. This wasn't a date after all. It was just a coincidence. Practicality. She needed my help, and I was helping her. Nothing more. But when I slipped off my coat and laid it over the back of my chair, her eyes lingered on my arms. She reached across the table, pointing.

"Did you design these yourself?"

I looked down at my forearms. Above my left wrist was a dandelion, on my right wrist a nautilus shell. "These? Yes, actually."

"They're beautiful." Her finger lingered close to the softest part of my forearm, but she didn't touch.

"Thank you. Do you have any ink?"

She perked up as if surprised by the question. "Me? Never. I couldn't."

"Why not?"

"I don't know. It seems like a big commitment. It's so..."

"Permanent?"

"Yes, exactly. I just can't imagine looking at the same thing over and over again, every day for the rest of my life. I think I'd get bored. Not that your tattoos are boring because they're not. They're quite beautiful. But for me, I don't know. I don't think I could pull it off."

"Pull it off?"

"I don't have the image for it. I'm a professor, first of all. A scientist. I barely even wear jewelry."

"Let me stop you right there. You could pull it off."

"You think so?"

"Well, I wouldn't recommend full sleeves or anything like that. At least not right away. But maybe something more subtle."

She leaned closer, crossing her arms on the table and smiling. "Any suggestions?"

"Suggestions?"

"Yeah, on what kind of tattoo I should get."

I reached across the table. "May I?"

She nodded and blushed as I reached for her hand, turned it over, and cradled it in my palm. I ran my thumb along her wrist. "Here. Something small. Something simple but meaningful. I could do it in less than an hour."

She watched my thumb, her lips slightly parted, her brows furrowed in concentration. "In less than an hour?"

"The actual tattooing, sure. But the hard part is deciding what you want. After that, it's just anticipation."

She swallowed hard and gently slipped her hand from my grasp. She looked around the room, suddenly aware of her surroundings. For a moment I thought she might comment on the other patrons. They were mostly women, after all, which was no surprise to me. That was the reason I'd brought her here in the first place. But if she did notice, or if she thought it was strange, she never let on. "Look at us. Been here chatting away and we haven't even ordered drinks yet."

"Of course," I said. "What are you drinking?"

"I don't know. You've been here before. What do you recommend?"

"Wine is very autumnal."

She nodded and smiled. "So it is."

I set my phone face up on the table. "Here, just in case Leighman texts. The passcode is 4422."

"You're not supposed to tell a stranger something like that." She reached for the phone anyway.

"Well, we're not strangers anymore. I'm Christina, and you're Justine. You're over, and I'm under."

I left her alone at the table, but I could feel her eyes follow me across the bar. I only turned back once—right after ordering our drinks—and our eyes met. She didn't look away or appear surprised. She smiled and tilted her head. A flush of warmth spread through me, originating in my chest and spreading lower, rather than the other way around. I smiled back, and before I knew it, I gave her the smallest wave of my hand. She leaned forward, resting her chin on her palm, and waved back with just the tips of her fingers. It was such a small, delicate gesture. I almost thought I'd imagined it. She looked tired but not bored, content but not entirely comfortable. For a moment I felt bad for her and wondered if Leighman would ever respond, or if we'd be stuck out here all night.

I carried our drinks back to the table. "Any messages?"

"Not that I noticed."

I slid her glass across the table. "Well, if we don't hear from him by the end of this drink, we need to think of a plan B. Don't you have anywhere you can go? A friend's couch you can crash on?"

"Yes, I suppose so, but it's already so late. I would hate to put someone out."

"Nah! These things happen. What are friends for if not for nights like this?"

She sighed and raised her glass. "To new friends."

I raised my glass, too. "To new friends." But after we touched glasses and each took a sip, I couldn't stop myself from adding, "Is this your way of saying you want to crash on my couch?"

She laughed. "I'm sure you have a very cozy, stylish couch, but no, I wasn't implying that."

"I would offer it to you, but I live so far away, practically in Oakland. The Uber back home would be a bitch."

"No, no, I couldn't. You've done too much for me already. Your kindness..." She looked down at her hands. "I fear that I don't deserve it."

"What?" I was taken aback by her sudden seriousness. "Why not?"

"Well, you see, I complained about you to Leighman. Not about you specifically, because I didn't know who you were, but I complained about the tattoo parlor. I was having a bad week, and I sent a nasty email, and I hope I didn't get you in too much trouble."

I leaned back in my chair, feigning surprise and indignation. "The noise complaint! That was you? Okay, that's the end of this friendship."

She hid her face in her hands. "Yes. It was me, but just try to see it from my perspective. I live right above you, every night I sleep above you, and I can hear you down there beneath me."

A string of images crossed my mind...*you above me*. I imagined her in a T-shirt, leaning on the kitchen counter. I imagined her home after a long day, discarding her cardigan in a darkened living room. I imagined her on her bed, not with one of the lovers I'd seen her take home, but alone and unselfconscious, perhaps with a book or her phone.

"What did you hear, exactly?" I said.

"Music mostly. But sometimes I'd hear your machines or people's voices—people crying or screaming."

"Shit, you make it sound like a dungeon."

"And when people are hanging out on the sidewalk or in that little back alley, I can hear every word they say."

"I get it," I said. "The last thing I want is to inconvenience you. As soon as Leighman gave me the complaint I made some changes. No music past ten, no smoking in the alley."

"Oh god! I forgot about the smoking! I could never leave the windows open. The smell was so bad."

"Gross! I'm surprised you put up with it for so long. And I'm glad you said something because it made a positive change in the world. Well, at least in the community."

"Yes," she said. "Things have gotten better, so I appreciate that. I can even leave my window open… wait a minute…" She reached across the table and grabbed my hand. "My window! It might still be open! We need to get to that alley."

"Easy," I said. "We can go right through the shop and out the back."

She looked down at our clasped hands, then at the full wine glasses. "But we've barely touched the wine."

"That's all right." I pulled my hand away as casually as possible. "The sooner we see about that window the better."

As if to prove my point, a rip of thunder rumbled overhead, causing the bar to grow momentarily silent. We hurried into our coats and out the door. Outside, a light drizzle floated on the air, but by the time we ran up the street and arrived at the shop it had already grown into pitter-patter on our shoulders. Justine shrieked behind me as I fumbled to get the key in the front door.

Once inside, we moved silently through the darkened shop to the door in the back hallway. I pushed it open, and we both groaned. The pitter-patter was now a shower. We stood in the doorway, facing one another with our backs against the door frame.

"It might pass after a few minutes," I said.

"Or we might be stuck here for a while." She rubbed her temples. Again, I could tell she was tired.

I poked my head out and looked up. My face and hair got soaked in an instant, but it didn't matter, I'd seen what I needed to see. I ducked back into the doorway. "Your window is open! And there's a fire escape. Did you know there was a fire escape?"

"How else did you think we'd get in?"

"I guess I hadn't thought that far ahead." I poked my head out again. The ladder to the fire escape was pulled up. The bottom rung was about ten feet off the ground. I ducked back in. "Bad news, though. The ladder is out of reach."

She glanced around the hallway. "Do you have an umbrella in here somewhere?"

"Sure," I said, but I wasn't sure how that was going to help. I went to grab one anyway.

When I came back, she took it from my hands. Without opening it, she stepped bravely out into the storm. She was instantly soaked. Her curls fell flat and dark down her face, and her coat looked twenty pounds heavier on her shoulders. Still, with a quiet determination, she walked to the little cinderblock wall and climbed up onto it. From there she stood up with the unopened umbrella in her hand. She lifted the handle of it up, stretching as far as she could, before catching the bottom rung of the ladder with the curl of the umbrella handle. She leaped to the ground, umbrella still in hand, and pulled the whole ladder down with her.

I stood in the doorway in disbelief. She walked back to me, barely able to keep her eyes open beneath the torrent of rain. She smiled and licked the rain from her lips as she handed the umbrella back. "Merci."

"You're welcome."

I don't know if she heard me, as she suddenly turned away and started to climb the ladder. When she got safely to the top, she looked down at me. "Well! Aren't you coming up?"

"I think I should get going!"

"But I owe you a drink."

"I couldn't."

"You'd be doing me a favor. I don't feel safe staying alone. Someone out there has my address and my house keys."

I hadn't thought of that. I set the umbrella aside, stepped out into the rain, and locked the door behind me. When she saw that I was coming up, she climbed in through the window. I climbed up the wobbly ladder. She reached a hand through the open window to help me, and I stumbled over the window ledge straight into her arms. We clung to each other in the middle of her kitchen. A heartbeat passed between, and then we both laughed.

"You okay?" She leaned back to get a better look at my face.

I looked up at her. Little raindrops still rolled down her cheeks as if they were tears, but her eyes were bright, and her cheeks were perky with joy.

"Yeah, I'm fine. A little wet though." Her cheeks reddened, and I immediately regretted my words. "I mean, my clothes are wet…from the rain."

"Here!" She hurried away and returned with a handful of fluffy towels. She piled them on the counter, then grabbed one. I'd expected her to dry herself first, but she wrapped it around my shoulders instead.

"Thank you." I slipped my shoes off, and without thinking reached up under my skirt and pulled down my leggings. I left them in a puddle on the kitchen floor. When I looked up, I saw her watching me from beneath her towel. I stood up straight, not sure what to do next. She dabbed her hair, then picked up another towel and laid it over my head. I disappeared beneath a curtain of soft terrycloth. She rubbed my neck and ears until the towel opened up and she held my face in her hands. She smiled down at me as she wiped the rain from my cheeks.

I leaned up as she leaned down. I closed my eyes. She held my face. Our lips touched. She tasted like wine and rain. The kiss was brief but warm, and I swallowed the feeling of it, letting it heat me up from inside. I opened my eyes.

"I'm sorry," she said as she took a step back. "I don't know what came over me."

"Don't be." I slipped a hand behind her neck and pulled her close. "I wanted it."

And it's true. I'd wanted her for a while now, but that want was hot and frustrating, originating from lust and curiosity. I hadn't expected this kind of want, softer and warmer, as intimate as her hands on my face. I hadn't expected her to be so lovely.

She kissed me again as she pushed my coat from my shoulders. I let it fall on the floor. Then, with a strength I hadn't expected, she grabbed me by the waist and pulled me closer. Her kisses grew hotter, more urgent. I leaned into them. I leaned into her, feeling small in her arms and safe. Distantly, I thought it was strange that I should be the one to feel this way, that I should be the one to melt into her arms like some damsel, and yet here we were.

She picked me up, and without thinking I wrapped my legs around her waist, a thing I'd never done or even imagined myself doing. She carried me down a narrow hallway to the bedroom, and we tumbled down onto her bed, laughing as we landed roughly, me on my back and her above me. I think the fall knocked the wind out of me, or maybe it was the sight of her—her cheeks flushed pink and her lips pinker—breath or no breath, I sought her lips again and again.

She reached down, pulling up on the bottom of my dress, but it wouldn't budge. I reached for the fly of her jeans but once opened, they wouldn't budge either. We both grunted and shifted and stretched, but it was pointless. I gave up on her jeans and moved up to her shirt. I lifted it up, and as it peeled away from her body, it made an unflattering suction sound. THWOP! She raised her arms anyway, but the shirt got caught around her elbows, leaving her stuck with her arms straight up in the air and her face hidden behind wet cotton.

"Oh my god. I'm so sorry!" I sat up straight and helped her wiggle out of the shirt. Finally, she appeared, her arms red from the exertion, her hair somehow both wildly frizzy and plastered flat to her forehead. Our eyes met, and I felt the need to apologize profusely, but then she broke out into laughter, and I couldn't help but laugh with her.

"This is impossible," she said.

"Totally. We should give up now."

She sighed and pulled me closer, kissing my

mouth. Then she grabbed hold of my arms. "You're shivering!"

"Am I?"

"Yes! This is madness. We're both going to end up with pneumonia. Let me get you some dry clothes."

I hesitated, but only for a moment, because I was freezing and soggy, and at that moment a dry pair of clothes sounded better than sex. "Thanks."

She left and came back with a T-shirt and some sleeping shorts. Then she led me to the bathroom to change. When I turned the light on and closed the door, I was horrified to see that street muck covered my legs in the pattern of my leggings. I wondered how much of the dirt I had left smudged on her bed. I pulled open the door and popped my head out.

"Do you mind if I hop in the shower quick?"

"I don't mind at all," she called from the hall. "There are clean towels in the cupboard."

I undressed and stepped into the shower, happy that the hot water worked better here than it did in the shop downstairs. I tried not to stare, but I couldn't stop myself from noticing all the little things, like the line of bottles along the window, all different colors, shapes, and sizes. I picked each one up and sniffed until I came to the one that smelled like her. It was a body wash, and I scrubbed myself with it. When I was done with the shower and dried off, I slipped on the shorts minus my underwear. I tried not to think about that too much.

I hung the towel back on the rack and laid my heavy, soggy clothes over the side of the bathtub to dry. I glanced at myself in the mirror and winced at the lack of eyeliner. I felt exposed and vulnerable without it. I was in a stranger's house, after all, sober and without underwear. Perhaps my lack of eyeliner wasn't so important.

I sighed and turned off the light, and when I stepped down the hall to the bedroom, I was relieved to see that the room was dark save for the flickering blue light of the TV on the dresser. Justine was laid out on her bed with her back to me. I assumed she was watching the TV, but when I stepped closer, she rolled over with a start, not seeing me by the bed.

"Christina?"

"I'm here."

She pulled back the covers. "Come on."

"Oh, I thought I'd stay on the couch."

"Don't be silly." Her eyes were barely open, but her tone was insistent. "There's plenty of room. Besides, the couch is *merde*."

I wasn't quite sure what that meant, but I think I got the idea. I slipped under the covers behind her. When she was satisfied that I wasn't going to leave she laid her head back down. She passed the remote to me behind her back, mumbling over her shoulder, "Watch what you want."

She fell asleep right away. Within minutes I heard the soft nasal puffs of her breaths. I, on the other hand, had a hard time falling asleep. I couldn't relax, not with her so close to me. I was uncomfortable and aroused but also concerned about what she'd said outside. There might be a stranger out there with her keys and address, and that thought alone kept me flinching at the smallest sounds. She never stirred next to me. Finally, I turned the TV off and watched the shadowy curve of her back as she breathed in and out. Despite my pounding heart, I slowly fell into line with her breath, until I grew sleepy myself. I fell asleep curled on my side behind her, but not touching.

When I woke in the morning, she was facing me. She smiled and brushed the hair from my face. For a moment, I was startled and out of sorts. But I hadn't forgotten where I was, not even in my not-quite-asleep dreams. I knew exactly where I was, and I was relieved that the night had passed and we were both safe, and the sun was rising outside, and the rain had stopped.

"I stand corrected," she said.

"About what?"

"Back at the bar, I said I couldn't stand to see the same thing every day for the rest of my life, that I'd get bored. But I think I could get used to this."

I hid my face in the pillow. "We were talking about tattoos."

"I know." She grabbed my hand, looking again at the dandelion seeds that floated up to my wrist. "Was it painful?"

"Yes, but the pain is temporary. When it's gone, you have this beautiful memory."

"Ah-ha." She ran her fingertip along my skin. "A memory of what?"

I thought for a moment. "Well, I can't tell you."

"Why not?"

"That's like telling your birthday wish before blowing out the candles. If you tell the secret, then the magic is lost."

"Ex-lovers?"

"No," I said. "Nothing like that."

"So you've never gotten a tattoo like that?"

"Like what?"

"You know, for a girl?"

"No, I'd never get a tattoo for a woman. I've seen too many regretful customers walk through my door."

"That's funny." She turned away, gazing up at

the ceiling as she continued to stroke my arm. "I think it's the only reason I would ever get one."

She hopped out of bed and headed down the hall before I could ask for more details. She made me breakfast that morning and several mornings after. Our romantic autumn turned into a San Francisco winter. We passed more than a few thunderstorms huddled together in her bed. Once spring arrived our romance was still in full bloom, and I'd learned many things about her like how she takes her coffee and how she shakes like a leaf when she's on the verge of orgasm. Summer was a blur of mornings passed in her little kitchen and nights on the fire escape, sharing glasses of wine and stories of the day.

One stormy evening in autumn, I was in the back office getting ready to close up the shop. I heard the little bell at the door, so I poked my head out to see who it was. I hadn't expected Justine to stop in. She usually went straight up to her apartment, but there she was, standing by the door, gazing up at the artwork on the walls like she had the first night we met.

"Hey," I said. "Give me five minutes. I'm almost done."

"Take your time. I'm in no hurry."

When I was done closing up, I snuck up behind her and wrapped my arms around her waist. "See anything you like?"

She smiled. "Do you remember what you said about my tattoo?"

"Your tattoo? I thought you said you weren't the tattoo type?"

"You said that it should be something simple but meaningful. I think I know what it is now. Do you have a pen and paper?"

"Sure, here." I grabbed a notepad and marker from a nearby table.

She leaned over and quickly sketched something on the pad and handed it to me. She'd drawn a simple skeleton key, like the kind you'd see in old Victorian art.

I looked up. "A key?"

"It reminds me of you."

I blushed. "Why?"

"The night we met, I'd lost my keys." She paused, hesitating.

"Oh." I nodded my head, trying to be supportive.

"You think it's too literal."

"No, not at all…"

"What I mean to say is, that night, I lost my keys, but what I found was something much better…I found you."

I blushed again, but only for a moment before I pulled her into a kiss. A year had passed, and I still felt like I was discovering her lips. I didn't want to stop kissing her, but she pulled away.

"So, you'll do it?" She raised her wrist to me.

"I don't know. It's a pretty big commitment. Besides, you already shared the meaning of the tattoo. It might lose its magic."

She kissed me again. "Somehow I doubt that."

L.K. Early is a graduate of the Golden Crown Literary Society's Writing Academy, Class of 2017. She has a passion for sci-fi, romance, and ghost stories, though not necessarily in that order. Her short stories can be found in Haunting Muses (Bedazzled Ink, 2016), Conference Call (Bella Books, 2017), and A Heart Well Traveled Volume 2: Tales of Erotica, Fantasy, and Sci-Fi Love Affairs and Unlikely Outcomes (Sapphire Books, 2017).

A Harlequin Gesture

By Gandara Gallishaw

Ally spots the blonde in the red and black corset from across the convention room floor. She is carrying a bat thrown over her left shoulder, laughing at something one of her companions said. The woman has her blond hair flowing down her back with the ends dipped red. Ally can't pull her eyes away, taking in the way the corset accentuates her ample cleavage. As if feeling Ally's eyes on her, the woman turns her head and their gaze's meet. A smirk flits across the woman's face, and Ally feels her cheeks burn at having been caught staring. The woman gives her an appraising look. Suddenly feeling self-conscious, Ally glances down at her midriff-baring green top and tight green spandex leggings. When she glances back up, the distance between the two is significantly less as the woman stalks across the floor towards her. Her gait is confident, and her smirk is still firmly in place. Ally isn't sure if she's committed to her character or if she just knows she looks hot. She feels like prey under the woman's intense gaze.

"See something you like?" the woman asks when she reaches Ally, voice husky.

Ally's eyes widen, staring up at the woman's piercing green orbs. She opens her mouth to respond and when no words form she closes it, feeling embarrassed in front of this beauty.

"I'll take that as a yes," the woman says extending her hand, "Lindsay."

Finding her voice and taking the offered hand she says, "Ally."

"She speaks," Lindsay says, smiling and lowering her bat to cross her hands over the top of it.

"Sorry for staring," Ally says, missing the feel of the woman's hand in hers.

"No need to apologize. I appreciate when a pretty woman is interested."

"What makes you so sure I'm interested?" Ally asks, suddenly feeling confident.

Lindsay quirks an eyebrow and takes a step closer. "Well aren't you?"

The heat between the two women is palpable. Ally's heart hammers in her chest as Lindsay looks at her like she could devour her. She isn't sure that she'd even resist. Their breaths mingle as Lindsay leans in subtly, tempting her, daring her to come closer.

"Ally!" a voice calls, shattering the moment.

Stepping back, Ally turns to see a woman standing at the entrance to a panel room looking at her expectantly.

"My sister, Sara," she says.

"Ah," Lindsay says nodding before a devilish grin spreads across her face. "Mind if I join you?"

Not wanting to say yes right away, she asks, "What about your friends?"

"I'm sure they can manage without me."

"Then follow me."

"With pleasure."

They quickly make their way to the waiting woman. Sara cuts Ally a questioning look as she takes in Lindsay.

"Sara, this is Lindsay," Ally says.

Sara waves and Lindsay nods in return. She steps around the sisters and opens the door, gesturing for them to enter. Sara smiles her thanks and Ally is quick on her tail before Lindsay follows them in. Ally sees Lindsay fall into step next to her as a hand lands on her lower back. She looks up at the taller woman, and Lindsay shoots her a wink. Sara takes her seat with Ally seated in the middle between her and Lindsay.

The room is full and loud with excited fans chattering amongst themselves about the sci-fi show at the center of this panel. Not much a fan of the show, Ally feels unsure seated between the two women. A hush falls over the crowd when the lights go out, and the stage remains illuminated as the host comes out and welcomes everyone. The people settle after the last cast member is brought out and everyone directs their attention to the front of the room.

As the crowd laughs, a hand falls onto Ally's thigh. She glances at Lindsay who is staring ahead. Ally tries to ignore the woman, and focus on the panel until Lindsay's hand slowly creeps up her thigh. Ally quickly checks to make sure her sister's attention is on the cast. Satisfied, her eyes close, as she enjoys the contact.

"You never answered my question," Lindsay whispers, breath hot against her ear.

A shiver runs through Ally. "What?"

"Are you interested?"

"Yes," Ally says shakily.

"Good," Lindsay says.

A nip on her ear has Ally gasping, fist clenched in her lap, fighting to hold in the moan that is bubbling in her throat. Her eyes fly open, and she discreetly looks around to see if the noise alerted anyone. Everyone seems to have their full attention on the cast at the front of the room. Ally releases a shaky breath. It's a few minutes before she feels Lindsay shifting beside her.

"What are you doing?" Ally says quietly.

"Just getting comfortable," she says as she moves her hand from Ally's thigh and brings it around to rest on her back. She leans into Ally and drops gentle kisses on her neck as her other hand takes purchase of Ally's thigh and kneads softly.

Ally feels conflicted. She's not a person that would let a woman she's just met touch her like this, especially not in a room full of people. Lindsay nips her again. *Fuck it. There's a first time for everything.* She pushes the apprehension aside and relishes in the attention being lavished on her by the other woman. The hand on her back is soft as it traverses the expanse of territory there. The other hand on her leg finally slips between her closed thighs. Her eyes roll to the back of her head just knowing that Lindsay can feel the heat trapped there.

She parts her legs ever so slightly, and Lindsay's hand begins a gentle massage over her leggings. For a moment, Ally curses herself for not deciding on the green skirt when choosing her costume. She is unable to dwell for long as the gentle massage between her legs begins to arouse her. Slowly Lindsay adds more pressure. Ally's sure her excitement has seeped through her clothing as she teeters on the edge of her release. Ally grabs Lindsay's leg, needing something to hold onto as the coil in her belly winds tighter. Her mouth falls open in a silent scream as her body reaches its peak.

Lindsay continues a light massage over Ally's center, helping her ride the subsiding waves of her silent orgasm. Suddenly, the lights come on, and the crowd erupts in thunderous applause. The panel is over.

Lindsay slips her hand from between Ally's thighs and breaks away from her neck, leaving the hand that is gently stroking her back. Ally's chest heaves. She keeps her eyes closed as she tries to calm her pounding heart. She peeks an eye open and sees a satisfied smirk on Lindsay's face.

"Wasn't that great?" Sara asks as she gathers her things.

With a shaky laugh, Ally says, "You have no idea."

The women head for the exit. Once they're out of the room, they step off to the side to get out of the way of the people swarming out of the room.

"I was hoping we could go to the artist gallery next," Sara says pulling her crumpled map out of her pocket.

Ally looks at Lindsay who is leaning on her bat again. Lindsay tilts her head towards the elevators and Ally nods in agreement.

"Why don't you go on ahead and I'll catch up in a bit," Ally says.

Sara looks at her sister and the other woman. She takes in Ally's flushed cheeks and Lindsay's too innocent look. Understanding crosses her face as she replies, "Yeah, sure."

Ally watches as Sara disappears into the crowd. Lindsay holds a hand out to her, smiling. She takes the woman's hand and laces their fingers. Lindsay guides them through the throng of people to the line waiting to enter the elevator. The two women don't speak as they get nearer to the front. The doors open to their right and Lindsay slips them into the lift, pressing a floor as they get pushed to the back when more people pour in. Lindsay pulls Ally flush against her. Ally looks up into the woman's smiling face. Lindsay reaches with her free hand and brushes a stray strand of Ally's dark hair behind her ear. Ally blushes as she coyly bites her lip.

As the elevator ascends the crowd of passengers thins, but they remain chest to chest. The robotic voice of the elevator drones out a floor number, and Lindsay moves for the doors. Ally allows Lindsay to lead the way. Lindsay pulls them to a door and removes the key card from her corset. The women enter the room. Lindsay drops the key card onto the table and turns to Ally who is standing near the closet. Lindsay takes a few steps to Ally and wraps an arm lightly around her waist.

Lindsay peers into Ally's eyes, searching. The weight of the moment settles on Ally now that they are no longer shrouded in darkness. *Does she want this?* She takes in the searching green eyes of the woman who has been so dominating, yet so gentle with her. *Does she want this?*

"Yes," she breathes.

A hand reaches her chin and tilts her head up. Soft lips meet, her eyes flutter shut, and she melts into the contact. She wraps her hands around the woman's head and tangles her fingers in the blond locks as the kiss deepens. After a few minutes of heated kisses, Ally finds herself lifted off the ground. Instinctively, she winds her legs around the waist of the taller woman. She's carried to the bed and gently laid down. She slides herself up the mattress and with a single finger beckons her temptress.

Gandara is studying Criminal Justice at Georgia State University in Atlanta. Her goal is to continue to law school. She has always had a love of fiction. She hopes to be able to continue writing stories for queer women.

Other Anthologies by Sapphire Books Publishing

The One: Stories of Falling in Love Forever - ISBN - 978-1-943353-32-3

If lucky enough, we fall in love once in a lifetime.

Children's books and romance novels promise us an encounter with a beautiful, mythical love – a passionate lover that sweeps us off kilter and changes everyday life into happily-ever-after. In reality, most fall in love a couple of times throughout a lifetime. Yet, those relationships fail to fulfill the "forever" expectancy – they end. Still, we hope that love, true and eternal will embrace us. We hope that stardust will cover the banal when life becomes monotonous or loneliness grasps us too firmly when days fades to night.

Reading about love triumphant sparks desire for more than uninspired routine existence.

In The One, an assortment of writers chronicle the discovery of the one woman to share the rest of life's journey.

Everyone deserves happily ever after!

A Sapphire Collection - Our Stories Continue Vol. 1 - ISBN - 978-1-943353-49-1

We craft lives from memories, shared moments with others, and from our experience as beings in the world.

Our stories emerge from fashioning bits and pieces of life together with imagination and putting these ideas into words. As writers, we build worlds, give birth to characters, and hope to create a portal into a new realm, a place of communion of ideas, where fiction is alive in the mind of the reader. That's the joy of having others read our work. Our stories continue in the mind of the reader. Stories become shared spaces of strength, joy, personal insight, and where the individual loses herself for a while in an alternative realm of her own creation.

A Heart Well Traveled - Vol. 1: Tales of Long Distance Romance and Unlikely Outcomes – ISBN – 978-1-943353-89-7

Discover the many facets of romantic relationships as authors in volume one of, A Heart Well Traveled, unravel the trials and tribulations of long distance love affairs.

Each author, with their own unique style of storytelling, will leave the reader begging for more. Go from wild rides to gentle love stories, exploring the twists and turns lovers go through as they work to be together despite the distance between them.

Explore bonds beyond friendship, chance meetings, family drama, gender complexity, longstanding love and unexpected passion as lovers seek their happily ever after.

A Heart Well Traveled is a collection of short stories where women who love woman share the joys and challenges of long distance relationships.

Can love really conquer all?

A Heart Well Traveled - Vol. 2: Tales of Erotica, Fantasy and Sci-Fi Love Affairs and Unlikely Outcomes – ISBN – 978-1-943353-95-8

A Heart Well Traveled - Volume Two: Tales of Erotica, Fantasy and Sci-Fi Love Affairs and Unlikely Outcomes. Each unique short story in this supernatural anthology will transport you to a magical interpretation of romance as authors bring to life, uncommon love affairs and out of the ordinary long distance relationships. Escape into the realms of eroticism, fan fiction fables, intergalactic intimacies, lunar love, mythical fantasy, and past lives revisited. Is it fate, is it destiny or is it one of those defining moments where the universe comes to a screeching halt as an epic love appears?

A Heart Well Traveled - Vol. 3: Tales of International Love Affairs and Unlikely Outcomes – ISBN – 978-1-948232-08-1

A Heart Well Traveled - Volume Three: Tales of International Love Affairs and Unlikely Outcomes. Love stretches across international boundaries as Sapphire brings you a collection of unique stories of romance and intrigue across the continents.

Pack your bags and let your imagination run wild as you find yourself on romantic escapes to Africa, Australia, Bora Bora, Canada, Europe, the Middle East, South America and the United Kingdom.

This fast-paced anthology will leave you wondering if you could endure love with nothing but miles between you and your lover. Watch as the characters face countless impossibilities without ever losing sight of the one thing we all want, one true love.

Can they defy the odds?